His presence loomed fro... permit me, I shall roll my knuckles along your back.

Heat flared instantly up her neck, but Gwen nodded, giving him permission.

When the first contact of his fist swept across her back, Gwen let out a moan. Pain and pleasure fought for dominance. She closed her eyes against the sensations of his healing and seductive touch, allowing her body to ease from its rigid position.

"Let your limbs relax," he urged softly.

"Feels so good," she mumbled.

He splayed his fingers and massaged the knots along the column of her neck. Delicious pinpricks trickled down her back, along with the melting snow on her head. Gwen knew she presented a wretched sight, but she gave no care. His fingers caressed the top of her spine and wove their way down to both shoulders. By the time he finished, her body was on fire with another type of ache, but her muscles had loosened up. There was no denying the man ignited a spark within her.

Gwen turned around slowly.

He placed his hand above her on the tree, trapping her against the rough bark with his body. Lowering his head near her ear, he whispered, "Better?"

The word had her breathing rapidly. Gwen did the unthinkable and pressed her cheek against him—his beard grazing her face. "Yes."

"Good." He breathed the word against her skin and withdrew.

He held her captive with the intensity of his gaze—compelling and magnetic.

Praise for Mary Morgan

"I loved every book in this series and highly recommend it."

~*Linda Tonis for The Paranormal Romance Guild*

~*~

"If you're looking to be transported to Scotland and Ireland, complete with a magical love story and one act of defiance which will shake the Fae realm for years to come, pick up *DESTINY OF A WARRIOR* today. Highly recommend!"

~*N.N. Light Book Heaven*

~*~

"Ms. Morgan does a seamless job of mixing historical, paranormal, fantasy, and time travel."

~*Still Moments Magazine, Between the Pages Review*

~*~

"This heartfelt fantasy romance is the stuff fantasies are made of and has readers sighing in envy and delight."

~*Stormy Vixen Reviews*

To Weave a Highland Tapestry

by

Mary Morgan

*A Tale from
the Order of the Dragon Knights*

This is a work of fiction. Names, characters, places, and incidents are either the product of the author's imagination or are used fictitiously, and any resemblance to actual persons living or dead, business establishments, events, or locales, is entirely coincidental.

To Weave a Highland Tapestry

COPYRIGHT © 2019 by Mary Morgan

All rights reserved. No part of this book may be used or reproduced in any manner whatsoever without written permission of the author or The Wild Rose Press, Inc. except in the case of brief quotations embodied in critical articles or reviews.
Contact Information: info@thewildrosepress.com

Cover Art by *Debbie Taylor*

The Wild Rose Press, Inc.
PO Box 708
Adams Basin, NY 14410-0708
Visit us at www.thewildrosepress.com

Publishing History
First Fantasy Rose Edition, 2019
Print ISBN 978-1-5092-2907-9
Digital ISBN 978-1-5092-2908-6

A Tale from the Order of the Dragon Knights
Published in the United States of America

Dedication

For my Dad.
Your shy "Gus-Gus" ventured out into the world and became a bestselling author.
Since I'm a firm believer there are libraries in Heaven, I'm positive you heard the news.
Thank you for watching over me.
Love you!

Prologue

When the ancient MacFhearguis clan settled near the Great Glen in Scotland, the Chieftain wished to bless the land, and his castle known as Leòmhann—*the lion*. Druids came from far away, bestowing their approval over stone, land, and people. Afterwards, they took part in a grand feast. Drink and food overflowed in the Great Hall. The bards recounted the tales of their Chieftain and his people while the children listened in rapt attention. Minstrels played songs of past triumphs, and the dancing and feasting lasted for countless days.

However, another tale lay buried within the stone walls of Leòmhann and only those brave enough could relate the true account.

And so, it was whispered there were those in the clan—weavers from an ancient order from the west—not happy with the Chieftain's refusal to offer a gift to the Fae who had graced his land before him. Or his lack of interest to take a wife from one of the tribes who followed their belief. Though he honored the old ways, the Chieftain deemed their requests a foolish act. He argued that the druids' blessing fulfilled their needs and hardened his heart against them.

On a cold autumn morn, he banished these irritating women to the forest, fearing they would weave ill thoughts amongst the other people.

Saddened by this act from their Chieftain, the

women grew concerned the Fae would not give their own blessing over this new land, leaving their people without a compassionate and wise leader. Regardless of his order to silence them, they sought another path to right this injustice.

Gathering around a bonfire on a moonlit Samhain eve, each woman brought with them one long golden thread from their looms. On a whispered prayer, they knotted them all together. Traveling deep into the forest far away from Leòmhann, they came upon a young yew tree. As they swayed softly, the women wrapped the knotted threads around the tree. After they were finished, they joined hands and sang out as one.

"*Seasons will ebb and flow—battles shall be fought.*

The loom of the land shall not see rebirth.

From left to right, the strands of time will knot and break.

Only when a weaver threads the true color on a winter full moon night, shall the land, stone, and clan be cleansed."

Smiling, they embraced each other, deeming their prayer had been received by the Fae. As the leaves rustled beneath their feet, none of them ever fathomed that the true master weaver to claim the heart of a MacFhearguis would not appear for over eight hundred years.

And as the centuries passed, the legend of the Yew tree became more of a curse, and the land around Leòmhann suffered.

Chapter One

Leòmhann Castle ~ Mid November 1209

"Ye do not torment me, so do your worst!" Patrick MacFhearguis raised a fist to the storm, daring the Gods to unleash more of their anger across the land.

From the parapet, he inhaled sharply as the icy, brittle rain slashed across his face and stung his eyes. His own anger surfaced along with the storm, as he contemplated the ongoing skirmishes throughout the Great Glen. "Did ye forget your own people, Gods and Goddesses?"

The wind silenced his shouts, and lightning splintered the sky above him. The elements were brutal and unfailing.

Drawing his cloak more firmly around his body, he studied the landscape in all directions. The thieving of cattle continued into the autumn months, leaving him and his brother frustrated. Many deemed the English King John sent soldiers in disguise to cause unrest throughout the land and to show the Scottish people their aging King William was weak.

Nevertheless, Patrick knew this to be untrue. King William had spies everywhere, including his elite group of warriors from the Sutherland clan. Though the king was old, the man still possessed a fierceness and commanding presence.

He chose to ponder another thought.

His clan and those of the MacKay—*Dragon Knights*—were one of the last strongholds in the Great Glen. King John had tried unsuccessfully to govern or impose his reign of terror within both clans.

Perchance the king fears the old beliefs and our ways.

Rubbing a hand over his beard, he squinted in the fading light of the day. "Aye, I ken 'tis the reason."

"Do ye always have conversations with yourself?" asked Alex, coming alongside him. "And why are ye shouting to the storm?"

Patrick eyed his brother skeptically while water dripped down his face. "What brings ye from the comfort of your solar, *my laird*?"

Alex shoved a large mug against his chest. "And here I was thinking ye were cold and brought ye some drink to take away the bite of the north wind and sleet."

Taking the offering, Patrick sniffed the contents. "Nae mead?"

His brother laughed. "Did ye not tell me ye wished to save the last jug Alastair MacKay made for Yule?"

"I had forgotten," admitted Patrick and took a swig of the wine. "I do not think there is much left."

"Nae worry. We have enough wine. Drink it quickly, before the rain waters down the good fruit." Alex pointed outward. "It has been several moons since any have attempted to cross our lands unwelcomed. Do ye sense a threat, and is this why ye dared to venture up here?"

Patrick spared a glance at his brother over the rim of his mug. "Nae. Only uncertain as to their cause."

"Ye must admit King John would consider it a

boon if he had the MacFhearguis and MacKay clans united with him, aye?"

"In truth, I deem he *fears* our heathen ways."

His brother nodded slowly. "I confess I had not considered that thought. Although King John's attacks were against the people and not the thieving of cattle."

Shrugging, Patrick took another sip of his wine. "Something to discuss with the Dragon Knights when we meet again."

"Aye, come spring," acknowledged Alex.

A clap of thunder resounded throughout the land, and both men glanced upward.

"I *could* take some men and retrieve more mead after the storm abates," suggested Patrick. "Snow is late in the glen this year."

His brother grunted a curse. "A blessing, if ye ask me."

"We'd depart in the morn. I do not foresee any issue with my absence here."

"Ye seem eager to leave right away."

Patrick studied his brother. "So, does that mean ye will let me go to Urquhart?"

Alex leaned against the stone, gazing outward. "Does the disquiet unsettle ye?"

"Always at this time of year," he confessed. Patrick gestured outward. "When the land becomes barren of leaves on the oak and other trees, I can see how nothing flourishes around Leòmhann."

"'Tis but a massive rock with trees. The land is too steep for anything else to take root." He dismissed him with a wave of his hand. "Ye ken this."

"Aye, *aye*," muttered Patrick.

"Your daily visits here are addling your thoughts."

Stunned by his brother's declaration, he turned toward him. "Are ye having me watched?"

Alex frowned. "Nae. But all can see ye up here, including me. Ye leave after sparring in the lists and stay until the gloaming. Ye pace *and* brood. Why is this season different than the others?"

The wine left a sour taste in Patrick's mouth. How well his brother knew him. Turning away from him, he responded, "I find solitude a welcome companion."

"What ye require is a wife."

Patrick glanced sharply at his brother with a horrified expression. "Never."

A great burst of laughter escaped from Alex. "Do ye find the chains of marriage too distasteful? If so, then take a woman to your bed."

He shuddered, shaking his head. "Aye, since I have stated I would not marry. And I have nae desire to be like our dead brother, Michael. Do ye not remember how long it took to beg any female from the village to cook for us after he died?"

"'Tis a blessing Tessa agreed and did not listen to the whispers of what others thought about us."

"She is aging but can manage a fine meal." Patrick swirled his wine, recalling how their older brother took many women, some even unwilling to his bed. Michael was feared by many, including him and Alex. Though the idea of bedding a woman stirred Patrick's lust, he sought none here.

Alex nudged him. "Ye ken I was not referring to the ways of Michael. With all he bedded, I cannot fathom why his seed never took."

"'Tis the Leòmhann curse." Patrick finished the wine in his mug. "Michael was not a good laird. 'Tis the bad blood of our heritage. With each new generation of kin, more problems arise."

"I do not fear curse words spouted from long ago. 'Tis poor leadership and his weakness for more power. As for our other brother, Adam, he *did* sire a son. How can ye explain it?"

Patrick gave his brother a skeptical glance. "Aye, we all share the same blood, but Adam's fate was *destined* with Meggie's to bring about a new order of Dragon Knights in another century. Adam's son, Jamie, is the future for the Dragon Knights. The Fae would dare not curse him, but their wrath might spill onto us."

Alex sighed and brushed a hand down the back of his neck. "True. We honor the Fae in our own way, though I must confess I miss our wee brother."

"As do I. I fathom he might have many sons by now," he mused.

"Or *daughters*," countered Alex.

Smiling, Patrick gazed outward. "With all this talk of bairns, why have ye not considered taking a wife?"

When his brother remained quiet, Patrick glanced sideways at him. A strained expression creased his features as he moved along the parapet. *What do ye fear, Alex?*

"'Tis not simple," his brother responded softly. "I ken 'tis my duty."

"What *clan* wishes to give their daughter to the Laird of Leòmhann?" demanded Patrick, striding forward. "Our lands are vast, but there are none that borders us who have any daughters."

Alex arched a brow. "Perchance I seek an alliance outside the glen. Have ye not pondered the idea?"

"By the hounds, nae! As I have expressed, I have

nae desire to take a wife." Patrick scrubbed a hand over his face. "Sorrow would be her companion here. I cannot fathom why ye would consider bringing another into this fortress."

"In truth, I would seek out clans who remained loyal to the old ways." Alex clamped a hand on his shoulder. "I shall rethink my decision when the snows have melted in the spring. For now, I give ye permission to leave in the morn and fetch more mead from the MacKays. Take two men with ye."

Patrick relaxed his stance as his brother released his hold. He smiled, grateful for the change of subject and his brother's decision to let him leave. "Thank ye."

Starting for the door, Alex paused. "Leave your foul mood out among the storm and think on taking a wife when ye return."

Patrick remained quiet until the door closed behind his brother. "Ye first, my laird."

****

With a renewed sense of purpose and longing to be out in the open land, Patrick skirted past a woman strolling along the corridor with an armful of rushes. He gave her a passing nod and made his way into the kitchens.

The heat and aroma of baking hit him squarely when he entered. Tessa was giving instructions to one of the lads as he struggled with a pail of milk in his small hands.

Reaching for a warm bun off the table, Patrick asked, "What provisions have ye packed for me, Tessa?"

She clucked her tongue in disapproval at the interruption. Ignoring Patrick, she continued to show the proper way to carry the pail without spilling its contents.

Leaning against the table, Patrick devoured the bun in two bites.

"I cannot hold with one hand," complained Hamish. "I must use both, or the milk will spill."

Folding her arms over her ample chest, she narrowed her eyes. "Did ye not spout ye could carry two pails to the other lads?"

The lad glanced down at his shoes. "'Tis not what I meant."

"Truly? The account was given in front of the laird. So whose tongue is speaking untruths? Ye, or our laird?"

Hamish snapped his head up. "Our laird *always* tells the truth." He swallowed visibly. "I forgot to add that when I am bigger, I will be able to carry two."

She tapped him on the head. "So ye *forgot* to mention those words into your boasting?"

His head bobbed vigorously. "Aye."

Tessa continued to stare at him, though mirth showed in her eyes.

"If ye wish to best the other lads, ye better start building strength in your arms," interjected Patrick. "Might I propose a solution?"

The cook gave him a doubtful glance. "Please do."

As Patrick pushed away from the table, he reached for another pail off a hook. Removing the full one from the lad's hand, he dumped half the milk into the empty one. "Mayhap ye can carry two now without spilling the contents?"

The lad's eyes widened. After taking both pails into his hands, he lifted his head with a renewed sense of determination. "Aye, I can."

He gave the lad a curt nod. "Good. Remember this lesson the next time ye spout something ye have yet to challenge. Do ye ken my meaning?"

The lad straightened. "Aye. I shall remember."

Patrick gestured behind. "Leave these pails and go tend to the rest of the animals."

They watched as Hamish scampered out of the kitchens.

"Thank ye," mumbled Tessa and moved toward the hearth.

"Were those words of praise?" mocked Patrick, reaching for another bun.

Keeping her back to him, she removed a spoon off an iron hook near the hearth. "'Tis only a grateful response to a lad I favor. And if ye snatch one more bun from the table, ye will get stale bannocks and no meat."

"Ye would not dare," he teased and deposited the bun back onto the table.

"Och, ye tempt me, Patrick MacFhearguis."

Chuckling softly, he asked, "Why do ye favor this lad?"

She shrugged. "Nae reason."

Patrick had his suspicions. The old woman had lost her husband at a young age and never remarried. When she arrived a year ago seeking the position of the cook, they learned she had no children of her own. Therefore, all those within the castle had become one of her favored children.

Hamish was merely another one added to her growing list.

Walking over to the hearth, Patrick peered over her shoulder. "Looks like a fine venison stew, Tessa. Ye are a good woman."

Her mouth twitched in humor. "Bah. Now leave me, so I can finish preparing the evening meal. Ye will find a leather satchel with food on the table by the herbs."

"Thank ye, *mistress* of the kitchens."

Her laughter followed him as he retrieved the bag of food and made for the bailey.

Smiling, Patrick lifted his head to the sunlight. A chill breeze swept past him, but the warmth of the sun filled him. His brother had asked for two of his guards to accompany Patrick, and he was relieved to see it was Andrew and Owain.

Both men gave him a nod in passing.

He approached his brother, who stood next to his horse. "Ye honor me by seeing me off."

"Merely making sure ye have enough supplies."

"How kind of ye."

Alex patted the side of Patrick's horse. "I meant for the animals."

"Ye wound me. Have I not always cared for all of them?"

His brother's mouth twitched in humor.

Quickly securing the satchel, Patrick mounted the animal. "I shall return by the full moon."

"Seven days?"

Glancing upward, Patrick replied, "I have nae desire to tempt the fates with our good weather. I hope to make it to Urquhart in two days ride."

"I say three," countered Alex.

"If I fail, I give ye permission to throw the first punch in the lists upon my return."

"Deal."

After giving one last salute to his brother, Patrick urged his horse downward along the steep path away from Leòmhann. Once they reached the bottom, he maneuvered the animal toward the bare birch and oak trees along the loch and gave the animal free rein across the dirt and leaf littered path.

A brilliant flash of autumn color burst forth from the trees along the edges of the water. The scenic beauty lifted his sullen mood, and he urged his horse onward.

By dusk, they were able to find a secluded area away from the water protected by thick pines. Dismounting from his horse, Patrick removed the satchel and water skins for the animals. After tending to the animals and securing them for the night, each man settled against one of the trees and ate their meals in silence.

Reaching for the wine skin next to him, he took a small sip. After wiping his mouth with the back of his hand, Patrick tossed it to Owain. "I shall take the first watch."

"Wake me in two hours."

"And me in four," responded Andrew.

Patrick brought the hood of his cloak over his head and rested his sword across his thighs. Stars glimmered through the heavy branches in the inky sky. An owl hooted, making its presence known to them and other night animals skittering about.

The heaviness within his soul he had fought these past few months returned as it always did in the evening. Clenching his jaw, he tried to banish the irritating emotion. He blamed it on the time of year when the bleakness of winter settled around their home, and how much they had lost in the past few years.

Nevertheless, his brother's words came back to haunt him.

I do not need a wife.

An owl hooted once again. Patrick lifted his head searching for the bird. Beady eyes shimmered back at him in the moonlight as if the bird wished to impart some great importance.

"I have sought no wisdom," he whispered. "Be gone."

With a great flutter of wings, the owl disappeared into the sky.

Too late, Patrick realized he might have listened to the messenger from the Fae.

Chapter Two

Leòmhann Castle ~ Mid November, Present Day

"I have a confession," announced Meggie, sliding her hand over one of the gilded tomes on the bookshelf.

Adam MacFhearguis slowly stalked his enchanting wife within the solar. "Do tell."

She brushed an ebony lock over her shoulder as she moved toward his massive oak desk. "Mayhap, I shall make you guess."

He arched a brow seductively. "Ye ken I enjoy a *good* game."

Chuckling softly, she leaned against the desk. "Ye mistake my meaning. 'Tis not a *sexual* game."

"Yet, they are my favorite," he admitted. "Give me a clue?"

Her cheeks turned a crimson shade, and Adam was drawn into her web.

Tapping a finger to her lush lips, she replied, "We are having a grand celebration in six months."

Adam paused in his pursuit. "Beltaine? We have always celebrated the feast day. Do ye mean it shall be grand, as this will be our first one at Leòmhann?"

She pursed her lips in concentration. "I suppose the event could happen then. But I was not referring to Beltaine."

Curious, he resumed his progress toward her.

"Another clue."

"More changes are coming."

When she tried to move away, Adam grasped her around the waist. "Good or bad?"

She tried to wiggle free from his hold, but he held her firmly. "Of course, it's good. These events are always good."

While he trailed a path with his tongue along the vein on her neck, she shivered beneath his touch. "Confess now or I shall take ye on my desk and ravish your body."

"Do ye not want another clue?" Her husky voice filled him.

"One more," he agreed, nibbling the soft spot below her ear.

"Our clan is growing."

Adam froze from his sensual foreplay and lifted his head. He blinked for several moments, trying to fathom the possibility. "Truly? Ye are with child?"

His question was answered with a radiant smile. "Aye."

Dropping down to his knees, Adam placed his hand over Meggie's womb. "Another son."

He heard her exhale softly. "As per our son's prophecy and the Great Dragon in the loch, we shall have two more sons after Jamie and Alexander. This will be our third."

Standing, Adam lifted his wife into his arms and sat down in his chair. Cradling her chin with his hand, he stared into her eyes. "I ken ye yearn for a wee lass, my love."

Meggie brushed a lock of hair out of his eyes. "Aye, true. Regardless, I shall love all my sons dearly.

And even a prophecy cannot predict the arrival of a girl."

"Then we shall keep trying." He sealed his vow with a passionate kiss.

Her moan resonated deep within him, and Adam deepened the kiss.

"I hope ye have locked the door, for I wish ye to take me here, husband," she murmured against his skin.

Before he had a chance to comply with her demand, a loud explosion shook the walls of the solar.

"By the hounds!" Adam immediately removed Meggie from his lap and ran to the window. Glancing in all directions, he did not detect any damage or the source of the intrusion.

"Great Goddess! What happened?" Meggie gripped his arm, attempting to look over his shoulder.

Turning from her, he went and retrieved his sword from above the mantel of the fireplace. "Stay here."

She gave him a scathing look. "Absolutely not."

Adam threw open the door to the solar and stepped into the entryway. "Lucas MacKay!"

Meggie's cousin sprinted forth from the library. "What the hell was that?"

When the first drop of water landed on Adam's head, he glanced up at the ceiling. "Sweet Mother Mary!" A jagged crack appeared in the plaster. "God's blood! 'Tis new!"

All three ran up the stairs to the third level. Racing down the corridor, Adam was unprepared for the sight that greeted him when he opened the door to his sons' playroom. The entire room had transformed into a swirling tempest of rain, wind, and lightning.

Fear took over his rage as Adam scanned the room

for his sons. "Alexander? Jamie?"

"I can't get him to stop!" Jamie answered somewhere in the darkened recess of the room. "He cannot harness the power."

"Sweet Brigid," gasped Meggie. She started forward, and Adam blocked her progress with an outstretched arm.

Lucas placed a hand on her shoulder. "I'll go forth and get them out."

Adam glanced warily at the man. "Can ye stop the storm?"

"Not until I find them first."

Adam drew Meggie to his side, allowing Lucas to enter.

She clutched at his shirt. "Lucas' power of the skies is not as strong as Alexander's. He may come to harm *or* destroy us all."

"Nevertheless, he is the only one who can stop this storm."

Rain continued to deluge the area, and now the water spilled out into the corridor. Moments ticked by in agonizing torture. He cradled Meggie's head against his shoulder. "If he does not appear soon, I shall go fetch them."

She trembled as lightning flashed, blinding them momentarily.

"Insanity," she hissed, and clutched at his arm. "I don't recall my brothers doing this much damage with their powers."

"Ye forget, beloved. Our sons are more powerful. 'Tis a new order of Dragon Knights."

A hushed silence descended all around them as the elements of the storm receded. When sunlight filtered in through a large empty window devoid of its stained-glass, Adam bit out a curse. The destruction of the room and possibly the entire floor from flooding was apparent everywhere he looked.

In a corner of the room, Lucas held their youngest, Alexander, in his arms. The tiny lad whimpered quietly against his shoulder. Their older child, Jamie, stood off to the side, his inner fire dragon showing forth through the amber color within the depths of his eyes. His fists were clenched at his sides as he glared at his brother.

Realizing the strength Jamie had to maintain to withhold his anger, Adam deemed it wiser to focus on the source of the disaster.

He brushed a kiss along Meggie's forehead, and handed her his sword. "Remove Jamie from the castle and send him to the loch."

"Do ye not think it best he spend some time in his chamber? As the oldest, he—"

Placing a finger over her lips, he shook his head. "Until we hear all accounts, he needs to rein in control of his inner beast *away* from here."

She swept her gaze toward her son and sighed. "We just finished this room."

Adam rubbed a hand down the back of his neck, attempting to ease the tension. "They both will help to clean this muck up *and* rebuild."

"I'm already dreading the day when all *four* of them wreak chaos." Meggie squeezed his hand and carefully entered the room.

Adam clasped his hands behind his back and gave Jamie a stern look as he retreated out of the room with Meggie. Returning his attention to his other son, he waited patiently for the lad to compose his emotions.

If he thought Jamie's fire dragon was a beast, nothing could have prepared him for the power of the sky dragon. Alexander had mastered the power of those elements swiftly in his early years and continued to expand, heedless to where he displayed his energy.

Lucas placed the lad on the drenched floor, and then gestured for Adam to step inside.

Hesitantly, Alexander trudged toward his father. Lucas gave Adam a curt nod before exiting the room. Though his son was young, Adam knew he had to make him understand the consequences of his actions.

"Explain," ordered Adam.

The lad continued to stare at the floor.

"Are ye not a Dragon Knight?"

Alexander jerked his head up. "Aye."

"Then why do ye cower in front of *me*?"

The lad's lip trembled as his eyes blazed. Adam realized his son had no control over the beast within his body.

"Does your dragon rule ye?" He gestured outward. "Did he order ye to bring forth the storm inside the castle?"

Thunder rolled around them, but Adam refused to relent. "I order ye to answer me—your laird *and* leader of the Dragon Knights."

Alexander swallowed. A mix of emotions were splayed across his tiny face—rage, confusion, indecision.

"I…got angry," he replied.

"And?"

"'Tis what happened."

Adam shifted his stance. "Is there more to your account?"

Wariness reflected within the lad's eyes. He jutted his chin out. "Nae. I will accept my punishment."

Adam considered there was more to his son's tale. "Until I speak with Jamie, you are confined to your chamber."

"It was not his fault," argued Alexander. He pounded his chest. "Mine."

I do not believe ye, son. The dragon's energy continued to swirl within the depths of Alexander's pale eyes. He placed a gentle hand on his son's shoulder. "Take a deep breath in and on the exhale, release the power of your dragon. Order him to withdraw."

The lad complied and shuddered on the exhale. His eye color returned to its normal shade of blue.

"If ye do not learn to harness your dragon when ye are angry, ye will be of no use as a warrior."

Alexander's eyes widened in shock. "I am sorry, Father."

"Go to your chamber. Think on your actions here today. We shall discuss this incident more later."

As his son somberly exited the room, Adam blew out a frustrated sigh. How he yearned to have the knowledge and wisdom of the past Dragon Knights, specifically, Meggie's brothers. She'd admitted she'd never witnessed this type of behavior, but he had heard the tales from his own brothers about the fearsome MacKay Dragon Knights when they were young. His own experience as a Dragon Knight began several years ago, so he had no wisdom to partake for his sons.

"Ye are all long dead and buried, including my brothers," he whispered.

His sons were powerful, dangerous, and so young. With another one in Meggie's womb, Adam required more assistance, or he feared Leòmhann would suffer at the hands of these future Dragon Knights.

Raking a hand through his hair, he gave one passing glance at the devastation and strode out of the room.

Approaching the loch, Adam noted Meggie speaking with Jamie near the water's edge. The lad had grown more in the past year and was nearing his mother's height. Although a lad of eight winters, he had the build of someone much older.

Their wolfhounds, Zeus and Odin, lifted their heads upon his approach as they sat by an oak tree. Adam signaled to both and they came to his side. "Go see to Alexander. I ken he could use some comfort."

The dogs sprinted off toward the castle, and Adam watched their progress. Returning his attention to mother and son, he waited until they were finished. After Meggie gave Jamie a hug, she quietly departed. In passing Adam, she brushed her hand against his. He returned the simple gesture with a smile.

Coming alongside his son, Adam cast his sight upon the loch. The soothing rhythm of the water lapping against the shore helped to ease the tension within his body.

"How severe is the damage?" asked Jamie.

Adam snorted in disgust. "Playroom destroyed. Do not ken about the other chambers on the second floor, and the downstairs ceiling is cracked and leaking."

"Shi—"

Glancing sharply at his son, he held up a warning finger. "Do not spout that curse word."

Jamie bowed his head. "Sorry, Father."

"Can ye give me your account?"

His son snapped his head up. "What did Alexander say?"

"He lost control of his anger," Adam spoke, though he knew there was more to the tale. *Will ye defend your brother or accuse him, Jamie?*

A smile came slowly to rest on his son's lips. "Loyalty."

"Excuse me?" Adam turned to face his son.

"As my second in command one day, Alexander proved himself worthy."

Fury burst forth within Adam, and he clenched his hands behind his back. "Who is the current leader of the Dragon Knights?"

Jamie frowned. "Ye are, Father."

Stepping closer, he glared at his son. "Then Alexander should have been loyal to *me* and answered truthfully."

"But he did, Father. He did get angry. His only crime was in not telling ye the entire account."

Turning from his son, Adam bent and retrieved a rock. "Why did he get angry?" Tossing the stone outward, he watched it skip nine times over the water.

"Amazing, Father."

Adam kept his gaze on the water. "Answer me."

"I enclosed him in a ring of fire," replied Jamie, quietly.

"Inside the chamber?"

"I warned him to hold back his dragon."

"So ye drew forth *your* power to show him a lesson? *Inside the castle?*"

Silence hovered in the air like an unwelcomed companion, and Adam waited patiently.

Jamie approached by his side. "Aye, but ye ken

Alexander is prone to angry outbursts."

"Ye are no better. As the *future* leader, ye showed no restraint. In truth, ye exercised your dominance over him. I expected more from ye, Jamie."

When Jamie remained quiet, Adam stole a glance at his son. Confusion marred his features. He had no more words to impart.

Both his sons erred in their judgment. Lessons required a firm hand.

Adam crossed his arms over his chest. "For the next month, ye will manage all chores alone—from hearth to stable. All training in the lists are halted—"

"How do ye expect me to learn—"

"Silence!" He cut his son's words off with a wave of his hand. "Ye have forgotten yourself. When I am speaking, ye will hold your tongue."

"I am sorry."

"Your day shall begin at dawn with chores. Furthermore, your lessons with Archie McKibben will be separate from your brother's. Until ye are worthy to assist in his training, I deem it wise to keep your lessons apart. Since Alexander is the younger, he will be taught in the morning and ye in the afternoons. Do ye ken my meaning? If not, ye can review the damage ye started and Alexander finished in the chamber and entryway."

Jamie nodded gravely. "Permission to speak?"

Adam relaxed his stance. "Aye."

"How…how did *ye* control your dragon?"

This is where Adam failed to have the wisdom to impart to his son. All he could offer was the truth. "As ye are aware, I did not ken about mine until a few years ago. My dragon was…dormant most of my life. When it did emerge, I battled the beast." He fought the smile forming on his mouth and picked up another stone. "In the beginning, I called my dragon a creature."

"Nae, Father, truly?"

This time Adam chuckled. "'Tis true. And I suffered greatly from the pain, too. Thankfully, my Fae warrior—"

"Conn MacRoich," interjected Jamie.

"Aye. He aided me those many months in the beginning."

"I have welcomed the training of Rory and Liam MacGregor," acknowledged Jamie.

"Two other great Fae warriors. Regardless, ye have yet to learn how to harness the power, instead of using it to your advantage. Ye are young."

"With time I shall learn. I will strive to be better, Father."

Adam turned and faced his son. Gripping him by the shoulders, he smiled down at him. "Your greatest challenge has yet to come. This is why we demand so much of ye."

Sadness passed briefly across his son's features. "I love ye, Father."

Embracing him, Adam whispered, "And I ye, Son."

Releasing him, Adam gestured Jamie back toward the castle. "Seek out your chambers and give me a guideline on the repairs."

"Ye trust me to assist?"

"I cannot let another fix what ye have destroyed."

Jamie snorted. "Nae, Father. Should we not ask Alexander?"

"Perchance. Now go."

His son sprinted off toward the castle, and Adam watched with a heavy heart. The future appeared clouded for his sons, especially with the burden of containing their dragon powers. They lived in a world vastly different from the one he knew as a lad.

"If only we were in the thirteenth century," he uttered softly.

As Adam slowly ventured back to the castle, Meggie approached across the bridge. She grasped his hands. "At least Jamie smiled at me as he ran past. Your conversation went well?"

He drew her against his body. "It started with harsh words but ended with good ones."

She blew out a sigh. "Good. In addition, Lucas is enlisting the aid of the other MacKays to fix the ceiling. He deems it should be completed in a few days."

"Leave the repairs to the chamber to me," stated Adam. "There are two young Dragon Knights who need to oversee this project."

Meggie wrapped her arms around his neck. "I have *another* confession."

Arching a brow, Adam feared to ask. "Should ye not be tending to Alexander?"

She smacked him playfully on the chest. "After his time spent in reflection. Do ye not want to find out what I have to say?"

"I do not think I can take any more surprises today. But if ye must, do tell."

"Remember my desire to have some tapestries made for the Great Hall?"

"Aye, I do. Can it not wait?"

Meggie leaned up and kissed him on his lips. "A master weaver skilled in creating these wonderful works of art is arriving here next week, and she'll be staying on with us until the completion."

Adam groaned. A stranger was the last thing they needed at Leòmhann.

Chapter Three

"You must weave with a steady hand and heart when you work the first stitch—be it on the loom or your destiny." ~Wisdom of the Elder Weaver

Gwen surveyed the massive stone structure from the inside of her vehicle. The gravel path curved upward, disappearing through thick pine trees. Her view of this part of the castle was stunning. The MacFhearguis flag billowed gently in the early morning breeze from the front tower. A parapet extended on either side, and she longed to see the rest of the stronghold.

"You are a medieval perfection," she uttered softly, resting her chin on the steering wheel. "And I haven't even started to explore you."

She had heard the rebuilding of this ancient fortress took several years. The structure mirrored the exact proportions as the original, or so many stated. While researching the Clan MacFhearguis in the archives in Edinburgh, there were no specifications, ancient drawings, nothing on the castle to use as a guideline. Apparently, this specific clan had knowledge from a personal—possibly only a verbal account of record, and Gwen craved to learn more.

Even in her small village of Abergale in Wales, rumors were rampant about the mysterious family living here and at Aonach Castle. Some whispered they worshipped the devil, and others argued they were merely pagan and honored the natural way of the land.

Gwen preferred to believe the latter.

When the order came in through her company for a chance to do an evaluation on making tapestries for the owners of the castle, she pleaded in her return email that though her business was small, she felt confident there wouldn't be a problem for her to oversee, create, and stitch the tapestry the MacFhearguis family required for the castle. Though the clan was considering another larger firm, they had been encouraged by her attention to detail and her habit of employing methods from centuries ago in order to complete a task.

Years of training had prepared Gwen for this job. In truth, no one else had the time or desire to challenge her for the position with the elusive MacFhearguis family, and they awarded her the contract.

The instant she pulled up a picture of the finished castle on her computer, her pulse beat rapidly. A sense of familiarity wove its way into her soul. Never in her life had she become so fixated on a place or project. After printing out the photo, she pinned it to the bulletin board above her desk. Her obsession demanded she take charge right away and prove to the MacFhearguis family that they made a wise choice when they selected Gwen.

Her first phone meeting went extremely well with Margaret MacFhearguis, and Gwen gathered everything she'd require for the important task of recreating epic pieces for the castle. Specifically, Margaret had requested one important tapestry to be finished in time for the Winter Solstice. Considering the deadline was seven weeks away, Gwen deemed she had ample time.

"No interruptions. No phone calls to answer. Only sitting at my loom and creating. Divine."

Soft bleating jolted her out of her thoughts, and she glanced to her right. Two lambs were in the nearby brush. One apparently had sustained an injury and was limping in circles.

Biting her lower lip, Gwen looked all around. No adult sheep and no person tending to them. Without guidance, out alone on the road they'd eventually make it to the main path and traffic. Traffic that could be deadly for the cuddly pair.

Spurring into action, she maneuvered the van off to the side and got out quietly. As she approached the two skittish animals, she crouched down.

Recalling the oatcakes in the pocket of her coat, she drew one forth. Crumbling it into bits, she then tossed them outward. The injured lamb continued with its mournful pleas, but its partner dashed forth and started to nibble on her offering. Gwen took the lamb's momentary reaction to move forward and scoop up the wee animal.

"What possessed you to journey out here without your mother, my wee friend?"

Securing the animal in the back seat of her vehicle, Gwen went back to the other lamb. Being careful of the leg, she gently lifted the crying animal into her arms and against her body. "Shh...little one. I'm positive someone at the grand castle I'm visiting can help you."

Pulling forth another oatcake, Gwen let the lamb nibble on the treat as she carried the animal toward her vehicle. After settling the baby next to her sibling, she swiftly got inside. Nevertheless, both little orphans began to bleat at a higher decibel than outside.

She started the engine. "Surely you can see I'm doing my best to help you."

Following the path upward, Gwen tried to block out her passengers' frightened looks and loud whining.

With each twist and turn of the road, the animals continued to utter their discontent at being confined. At one maneuver around the bend, they both slid across the seat, and she feared she was causing more harm to the one who was injured.

When Leòmhann appeared before her, Gwen's breath hitched. "There's even a portcullis." Her backseat friends were oblivious.

After crossing the bridge, she came up to the security box near the gate. Glancing upward, she half expected to see guards stationed within the tower.

Rolling down the window, she pushed the button.

"Miss Hywel?" A deep male voice came through the speaker.

Impressive! "Yes. I'm here to meet with Mrs. MacFhearguis."

The loud bleating from the lambs continued, along with a fight to get into the front part of the vehicle. She twisted around, doing her best to pacify them into silence, but to no avail.

"Did ye bring animals with ye? I thought ye were a weaver."

Gwen rolled her eyes, praying there wasn't a camera anywhere. "Yes and no. I'll explain when I get inside." For a brief second, she feared they'd turn her away.

Instantly, the portcullis raised, and she breathed a sigh of relief. Glancing over her shoulder, she glared at her companions. "My first impression is not going well, you two."

Returning her attention back to the road in front of her, Gwen drove the van through the gates and around a circular path leading near the entrance of the castle.

A stunningly beautiful woman emerged from the two massive oak doors, followed by an extremely tall and ruggedly handsome man.

Gwen smoothed the front of her dress and let out a groan. Dirt covered the front and side from rescuing her new-found friends. All she could do was give her new clients her best smile.

Exiting the vehicle, she thrust out her hand. "Hello, Mrs. MacFhearguis, I'm Gwen Hywel."

Taking her hand, the woman smiled. "Please call me Meggie." She gestured to her right. "This is my husband, Adam."

The man nodded. "Welcome to Leòmhann."

Meggie peered around Gwen with a puzzled expression. "Did ye bring your sheep to spin the wool?"

She bit the side of her mouth to keep from laughing. "No. I rescued them at the bottom of the road. One has an injured leg."

"Sweet Brigid!" exclaimed Meggie. "What were they doing so far away from the others?"

"Alexander is in charge of all the sheep this morn," declared Adam as he stepped past her. He opened the door to her vehicle and bundled the small animals into his large arms. Speaking to them softly in Gaelic, he beamed at her. "Ye are a kind woman to stop on your travels here to tend to the wee ones."

The man's smile was dazzling in the morning light. "I believe anyone would have stopped to help," she stated.

"Nae likely."

Meggie rubbed the top of their heads. "I'll send Alexander to ye after I get Gwen settled in her chambers."

Adam gave her a slight smile as he strolled away.

Gwen watched the exchange of her two employers. *Chambers?* The mere word had her senses tingling.

"It's a grand castle," she blurted out.

Meggie laughed, coming to her side. "Ye should have seen the ruins a few years ago."

"Shambles?"

"Worse. My husband doubted we could ever rebuild."

Gwen glanced at the departing hunk of a man. "I'm happy you proved him wrong."

"Most of the time I do."

Returning her attention to the woman, Gwen smiled. "Let me start unloading the van."

"Allow me to assist ye."

As Gwen went to retrieve her first piece of luggage, the stench of animal dung filled the inside. "No, *no*."

"Any damage?" asked Meggie.

"Only on the seats. This is a rental, so I'm going to have to pay a massive fee for repairs."

Meggie touched her shoulder. "After we're done, ye can take the vehicle around the back near the stables. We'll make it fresh again."

"You're too kind. I'd like to repay any costs involved." Though Gwen didn't know why she was spouting such nonsense. Every last dime went to supplies and the rental from the partial payment for this project.

Meggie waved a hand dismissively in the air and pulled forth a large garment bag from the back. "Do not fret. Ye are our guest and doing us a favor by creating the family tapestry."

Grabbing two pieces of luggage off the floor of the vehicle, she followed after Meggie. Upon entering, Gwen stared in awe at the entryway. Soft, golden light spilled forth from the candles along the stone walls. A stone stairway circled upward, but it was the stained-glass window depicting the coat of arms that caught her attention on the upper back wall. The lion faced forward with one paw placed on a large stone carved with Celtic spirals. A yew tree graced one panel, along with an oak on the other side. She never witnessed a more fascinating crest.

Meggie nudged her. "I see ye have noticed the family crest."

"*Leòmhann*," she whispered.

"Ye have studied the history?"

Gwen blinked. "Yes. I must confess I wanted to get a sense of the land and castle."

"Some say 'tis cursed here." Meggie glanced around the entryway. "We shall see that it flourishes, though the land is barren and farming or tending to animals makes it difficult. I can't even get roses to bloom on the southern side. My husband believes it should be blessed." She let out a nervous laugh and returned her gaze to Gwen.

"I tend to ignore folklore," she lied. The legend or curse of the Yew tree was often repeated by other weavers when they heard she'd applied for the contract. Contrary to what they believed, Gwen found it an interesting subject and dove into her research with relish.

"Many do not ignore the superstitions," remarked Meggie.

Gwen swept her gaze back to the flickering candles. "Do you have a problem with electricity?"

Arching a brow in humor, Meggie started forward. "My husband tends to feel more comfortable with keeping Leòmhann fixed on the past. The castle is wired for electricity in some parts, but not in the main entryway, Great Hall, and several of the chambers."

"Interesting," she mused, following slowly behind her hostess.

"Ye could say so."

"The medieval time-period is a favorite of mine," confessed Gwen.

Meggie glanced over her shoulder at her. "I can see why ye were so eager to take on this project."

Coming to the first floor, Meggie then led her to the left. Another set of stairs ascended on the opposite side, and Gwen longed to have a complete tour of the castle. The corridor dipped slightly to the right, and Meggie opened the massive door to her chambers.

"These will be your sleeping and working chambers. This one has electricity." She swept inside, adding, "The light is stunning from this chamber. As a weaver, I ken how important it will be. Your rooms face the morning and afternoon sunlight."

The scent of candles and flowers filled Gwen as she stepped across the threshold. A blazing fire filled the hearth on one side of the room, drawing her farther inside with its welcoming warmth.

She dropped her bag by the window and gazed

outward. "What a splendid view of the forest."

"'Tis magnificent in the autumn," added Meggie. "Your inner chamber is more personal and for sleeping."

Gwen stepped away and toward the secondary chamber. Another hearth set against the right wall. Yet, it was the huge bed that dominated the room, along with a giant armoire. Landscape pictures graced the surrounding walls, and she noted the large cushioned bench under the arched window.

She clasped a hand over her heart. "Goodness, it's beautiful."

Meggie tilted her head. "Then ye are pleased?"

"Absolutely."

"Perfect. I want ye to be at ease here at Leòmhann. After we get ye settled, I shall show ye the rest of the castle and surrounding grounds."

Gwen almost jumped in giddiness. Instead, she smiled broadly. "I would enjoy seeing everything."

Departing the room, Meggie continued to ramble on about Leòmhann, but Gwen had forgotten the most important question she burned to ask. "Meggie?"

Her host paused at the top of the stairs. "Aye?"

"What particular tapestry do you want completed by the Winter Solstice?"

Excitement flared within Meggie's eyes. "I want one of our family. I shall leave the background to ye. I'm showing ye as much of Leòmhann to fill the well of your creativity."

Curious, Gwen asked, "How many in the family?"

"Two sons and another on the way."

"You are pregnant? With a boy? I would not have known." The woman wore tight-fitting jeans and a lovely blouse, giving no indication of a babe. Gwen's knowledge of children was limited, but she believed you could not find out the sex of a child until four or five months.

Meggie chuckled and descended the stairs. "Call it a...*prophecy*."

Shrugging, Gwen followed her new employer out of the castle. As they pulled more luggage out from the back of the vehicle, she pressed her hand against a giant crate. "This will require strong arms. It's a major piece of my loom."

"I'll fetch Adam or Lucas—he's one of the MacKay cousins overseeing some work on one of the chambers."

Gwen's eyes lit up. "I heard about the MacKays of Aonach."

"Have ye?" Meggie flipped the handle up on a large piece of luggage and tossed another smaller tote over her shoulder. "Ye do ken I am a MacKay?"

Stunned, Gwen shook her head. "And ye married a MacFhearguis?" After removing two more work related boxes, she tried to keep up with the woman.

"So ye heard the ancient stories of the original feud between the MacKays of Urquhart and MacFhearguis clans?" asked Meggie, pulling her luggage up the stairs.

"Yes. But didn't they resolve their issues or whatever feud they had? Though I do recall history stating the MacFhearguis Laird was killed by a MacKay. Thankfully, peace finally was attained by the next laird, Alex, and his brother, Patrick."

Meggie paused. "Aye, eventually they did. It was a blessed day when all grievances were settled, and a truce was had by both clans." Sadness reflected briefly over her features, but she quickly masked the emotion.

Studying the woman, Gwen waited for her to proceed—either to her chambers or in the conversation.

Sighing softly, Meggie lifted her head to the stained-glass window. "This is why 'tis so important we have a tapestry of the family. I wish to have it hanging in the Great Hall over the hearth. It shall be a symbol of the bond between our clans. Perhaps then the legend of the Yew tree will be broken."

Gwen stared as her host moved quietly down the corridor. She had pursued the ancient tale, but that's where it ended. There was no mention of the legend or truce in any written records. Merely whispered words carried down through each generation of clans.

And then an idea blossomed.

"I'll break the curse for you, Meggie MacKay MacFhearguis. I'll weave you a stunning masterpiece to treasure forever."

Chapter Four

"Honor before thievery, unless the road means certain death." ~MacFhearguis Motto

Rubbing a gloved hand over his jaw, Patrick surveyed the terrain. If they continued on their present course, their travels would cost them another day. There was another path that would lead them to the edge of MacFhearguis and MacKay lands. Though more treacherous, they'd be able to arrive at Urquhart come early morn.

Andrew rode over to his side, glancing upward. "Are ye thinking of taking the path over the mountain?"

"For a hot meal and the comfort of a fire? Aye, most assuredly."

"'Tis nothing to do with the bargain ye made with the laird?" chided Andrew.

Owain approached on Patrick's other side and grunted a curse. "Nae, 'tis the bargain he made with his *brother*."

Patrick narrowed his eyes. "Ye both wound me. Here I thought ye sought the comforts of good food and warmth."

"Not to mention fine mead," interjected Andrew.

"Indeed. My sole purpose for the journey. And the sooner we get there, the sooner we can conclude our business." Patrick shifted on his horse. "Nevertheless, I would consider it a boon if I can return within the seven days."

"Did we not have a fine meal of dried beef and bannocks to break our fast?" Owain asked as he dismounted from his horse.

Andrew scowled. "Hard as frozen horse muck on a winter morn."

"But a meal. I offered to fetch some mushrooms and acorns." Fisting his hands on his hips, Owain turned toward the north.

"I have nae problem trekking upward," stated Andrew. "Can ye not hear my stomach protesting for more food?"

Owain waved a hand about. "Ye complain like an old woman. Ye had your meal an hour ago."

The man shrugged. "I can already taste boar meat and onions or salmon in dill sauce."

Closing his eyes, Owain sniffed the air.

Patrick let out a groan. The guard had previously trained under a druid and was skilled in signs pertaining to the land. He feared to ask the question. "Are ye forecasting an omen?"

Opening his eyes, Owain knelt on one knee. "Snow *is* coming."

"Lugh's balls," muttered Patrick, raking a hand through his hair. Indecision plagued him on whether they should return to Leòmhann. *All for some bloody mead.*

"I say we continue," suggested Andrew, glaring at Owain.

The man stood and folded his arms over his chest. "'Tis not your decision."

Patrick patted the side of his horse. "How long

until the first snowfall, Owain?"

He tapped a finger to his head in thought. "Perchance three days."

"Good. Then we shall take the northern path up the mountain. Our time with the MacKays will be shorter than I had planned." Patrick glanced at both men. "Are we in agreement?"

"For mead? Aye," affirmed Andrew.

Mounting his horse, Owain gave an exasperated snort. "And for a sample of the *uisge beatha*."

Patrick arched a brow in amusement. "Ye tempt fate with the Dragon Knights."

He shrugged. "Are they not our friends? Did ye not bring something to barter with as well?"

Nodding slowly, Patrick replied, "Ye ken I have some wool and wine to give to them."

Owain straightened on his horse. "With a wee amount of the liquid amber on our travels back home it will sustain us, particularly on a snowy day, aye?"

Patrick roared with laughter. "Perchance ye should be the one to ask Laird Angus."

"The fire dragon?" The man shook his head. "Ye are our leader, so ye can be the one to ask him."

Patrick's dealings with Angus were few over the past couple of years. Out of all the Dragon Knights to return to Urquhart, Angus was the last to arrive. Evil had woven its talons around the knights, each having to walk a path of redemption after the supposed death of their sister, Margaret by the sword of her brother, Duncan. Eventually, all four brothers returned home, only to find out she lived in the future. And now she was married to Patrick's brother Adam, who also resided in another century.

Furthermore, if anyone had asked him about the land dragon, Alastair MacKay, he'd had plenty to share. When his older brother, Michael was laird, his brother had imprisoned Alastair, along with his future wife, Fiona in the dungeons at Leòmhann.

Patrick grimaced, recalling the memory and how he was instrumental in securing the freedom for the MacKay and Fiona. An escape which cost Michael his life when he pursued the couple.

"Are ye contemplating returning, Patrick?" asked Owain, pulling forth his water skin and drinking deeply.

Andrew remained silent, choosing to keep his focus on the mountains.

"We must be in agreement," confirmed Patrick. "Andrew? Trouble ahead?"

"Unsure." He glanced sharply at him. "Can ye tell me about these dragons that dwell in each of the MacKay men? I have nae wish to offend *or* let lose their beasties."

Owain coughed into his hand. "Alastair is the land dragon. Duncan, the sky and storms, and Stephen, the water dragon. Ye have heard the account about the last battle with the evil druid, Lachlan, so why your question?"

Scratching his beard, Andrew replied, "Aye, but if we are spending time with these men, I judge it wise to remember the knowledge."

"The MacKays—*Dragon Knights* are our friends," declared Patrick. "Once, we were foes, but nae longer. *Remember* my words spoken here today. They are trusted allies."

"As we all honor the old ways, we hold respect for them," added Owain.

Ye would have made a great druid, my friend. Patrick gripped the reins of his horse. "Let us start forward. We have wasted enough of the daylight." Glancing sharply at Andrew, he added, "I can share more about the Dragon Knights come night, if ye have any further questions or worries."

Without giving time for either to speak, Patrick urged his animal toward the mountain and forest.

****

Early afternoon sunlight filtered in through the front doors of the castle. Shouting, followed by laughter echoed outside. Recalling her brief encounter with the MacFhearguis children last evening, Gwen imagined a new game was being devised by the oldest, Jamie.

After their evening meal, he brought forth his chess board and pieces, regaling her with a story of how he mastered the game. Intrigued, she encouraged him to teach her the rules of chess. The game proved something of a challenge, and Gwen told herself that one day she would learn the dynamics.

Jamie proved to be a skilled teacher. Though he achieved checkmate in less than one hour, he praised her on being a quick study.

Smiling, Gwen continued onward into the Great Hall. Warmth enveloped her from the blazing hearth at the back of the hall. Numerous candles set in wrought iron holders hung suspended from the high ceiling. Since their meal last night was served in the vast kitchens, she pondered what the atmosphere of the hall would be like when their wicks were lit.

Coming to a halt in the center, she took in the atmosphere of the place. Tables and benches graced both sides of the stone walls. In the center rested a longer one near the hearth—a bowl of apples graced the top.

As the fire snapped in the quiet hall, Gwen closed her eyes. If she listened hard enough, maybe she could hear echoes of past voices—filling the room with boisterous laughter and bards regaling tales of old.

Humming an old Welsh tune, Gwen tapped her foot.

"I like the tune," announced Jamie.

Startled out of her pleasurable thoughts, she opened her eyes.

Jamie leaned against one of the tables and folded his arms over his chest. He was a mirror image of his father.

"A lively melody from Wales," Gwen shared, moving toward the hearth.

"Were ye trying to get a sense of the hall in ancient times?"

You're inquisitive, young Jamie. "Yes. Your mother desires to have the family tapestry hanging in the Great Hall by the Winter Solstice. Before I begin any tapestry, I like to get a sense of the people, history, and land."

Jamie approached by her side. "And what have ye concluded?"

She tapped her finger against her mouth in thought. "I need more information."

"Have ye wandered around the castle?"

"Your mother was kind enough to take me on a tour yesterday."

His amber eyes lit up. "Ye must get a feel for the surrounding land. Can ye ride?"

"*Ride?*" she echoed.

"Horses."

"Oh. Absolutely. My uncle had me on a horse at three years."

Jamie tapped her on the shoulder. "Wonderful. Then ye need to view the land. Follow me."

"Isn't the terrain steep around here?" Gwen followed him, unsure if this was a good plan. "Perhaps on foot would be best?"

He waved her off. "Nae. We can take the back trail into the forest."

"*We?*" she squeaked, watching as he sprinted out the front doors and across the bailey.

Her plans to wander aimlessly inside and around the castle had now morphed into an adventure on horseback. And with a young boy. "Let's check with your parents before we venture out!" she exclaimed, attempting to keep up with his pace.

Finally entering the stables, Gwen paused against one of the stalls. "Did you hear me, Jamie?"

A cold muzzle nudged her from behind. Glancing over her shoulder, she gazed into dark eyes. "Sorry, but I don't think I should go riding with a young boy."

"I am older than ye think," he affirmed flatly, emerging forth with a horse trotting behind him.

She rolled her eyes as he brushed past her. "I think we need to discuss this plan with one of your parents."

"And I deem it wise for ye to move away from Dark Thunder's stall. He gets mighty mean at intrusive people."

Ignoring her further, Jamie secured the horse outside and proceeded to prepare another horse. "Do not worry. I will let father ken we are traveling out on the land."

Gwen moved away from the animal. It was useless to continue arguing with the boy. Apparently, he had made up his mind to escort her around Leòmhann. "There's one tiny flaw in your plan, Jamie."

He snorted. "Nae likely."

Gwen folded her arms over her chest. "These flat shoes will not suffice." She wiggled one foot out in front of him.

Chuckling softly, he dashed down the stalls. Opening up a large cabinet, he retrieved a pair of riding boots. Quickly returning to her side, he dumped them in front of Gwen. "Problem solved."

Bemused, she picked them up. "How do you know they'll fit?"

"I'm usually correct in my assessments of sizes."

What child talks this way?

"While ye get ready, I'll go tell father we are leaving."

Gwen gaped at the boy's retreating form. Slumping down on a nearby bench, she removed her small flats. When she shoved her foot into the boot, she almost wanted it not to fit, so to prove the arrogant boy wrong. Yet, it fit like a glove.

"You are a strange boy, Jamie MacFhearguis. Thankfully, I happen to like you."

After slipping the other boot on her foot, Gwen stood. She zipped up her jacket and walked out of the stables. Pausing at the door, she stole a glance at Dark Thunder. The sable coat on the horse glimmered in the dark interior. "I bet you're a gentle soul."

The horse let out a large snort and moved away from the gate of his stall.

Jamie and Adam emerged from the side of the

castle. Gwen watched the pair in awe of the similarities between father and son. They both possessed dark hair, same manner of speaking with their hands, stern expressions at times, and the stride in their step. The only difference was in the color of their eyes. Adam's reminded her of dark sapphires. However, Jamie's shifted with the many different hues of amber.

"Do they fit?" asked Jamie, giving a clicking sound to the horses.

Gwen moved in a small circle. "Perfectly."

Adam laughed, reaching for the reins of one of the horses. "I have instructed my son to stay within view of the castle." He pointed over her shoulder. "The view is remarkable from the edge of the forest. A good point of reference."

Jamie darted near the entrance of the stables and picked up a stool. Returning to her side, he placed it near her horse.

"Why thank you." Taking hold of the pommel, she stepped onto the stool and mounted the animal.

Adam handed her the reins. "Ye have the pleasure of riding Morcant. He has a gentle spirit."

After taking the reins, Gwen leaned forward. "A pleasure to meet you."

The horse shook its glossy mane, and she laughed.

"Return by dusk, Jamie," ordered Adam, giving a firm pat to his son's horse. "Water?"

"Aye," replied his son, pointing to the flask attached across the pommel on the saddle.

Adam started forward. "Allow me to open the gates."

Slowly nudging her horse onward, anticipation filled Gwen. Not a cloud in the sky on this brisk autumn day. Not to mention the surrounding scenery might provide some insight as a backdrop to the tapestry. As they reached the gates, Jamie waved to his father and took off across the bridge. He then veered to the right along a path leading toward the forest.

Following his lead, Gwen urged her mount to do the same. Soon they were galloping through the terrain. The wind slapped at her face, infusing her with reckless abandonment. The scenery soaked up the autumn glow, and she made mental notes of the surrounding colors.

Jamie kept his mount to a brisk pace for an hour, and then slowed as they neared the edge of the forest. Maneuvering his horse around, he waited for Gwen to join him.

"What an exhilarating ride," Gwen remarked. "I haven't been riding in a couple years, so I must thank you for recommending this, Jamie."

Beaming, the boy gestured outward with his hand. "Ye are welcome. But look at the beauty behind ye."

Turning slightly, Gwen gasped in awe. The rocky hillside was the perfect backdrop to the stunning castle. From her advantage, she was able to discern more details—the jut of the back fortress to the spectacular round tower in the front. Beyond, the sunlight cast its radiance on the loch in the far-off distance. The water appeared to have tiny jewels dancing off the surface.

She tucked a stray curl behind her ear. "Is that Loch Ness?"

"Aye and so much more."

Swiftly returning her attention to Jamie, she grew curious. "Do tell."

The boy appeared transfixed by the water. "*Magic.*"

That one word sparked an idea for her. Gwen peered over Jamie's shoulder. "Can you show me the yew tree?"

He blinked as if coming out of a trance. "Why?"

"I thought to weave the tree into the family tapestry."

He shifted on his horse. "I judge an oak tree would suit more."

Gwen refused to be deterred. "I do realize some say it's cursed—"

"Nae, merely waiting for the master weaver," he interjected.

"Excuse me?"

A look of wariness passed over his features. "Dusk is arriving soon."

Sighing, she moved her horse closer to his. "I don't understand what you mean, but we have a couple more hours of daylight. I only want to get a mental picture of the tree. Is it too far? We can always return tomorrow morning."

"'Tis not far, but the path narrows. We cannot take the horses all the way."

"Then let us proceed." She reached out and touched his arm. "I have my reasons." Though Gwen wasn't sure if her reason for forcing the issue was because of the tapestry or something else niggling at her senses.

He gave her a quick nod and swiftly dismounted. "Follow me."

Triumph filled Gwen as she got off her horse.

True to the boy's word, the path narrowed almost immediately. They secured their horses to one of the trees and made their way deep into the forest. Sunlight filtered through the thick canopy of branches, yet the area seemed to be devoid of birdsong and animals. Dead leaves crunched under their feet, and several times, she had to duck low under heavy limbs. The climb was arduous, and once she tripped over a tree root.

By the time they emerged near the yew tree, Gwen was breathing heavily and hastily unzipped her jacket. Wiping a hand across her brow, she lifted her gaze. An odd sense of familiarity swept over Gwen as she neared the massive giant. "You are magnificent."

Taking in the nuances of the bark, limbs, and leaves, she tried to commit to memory every detail. A flicker of light radiated off the trunk. Intrigued, Gwen slowly reached out her hand.

"'Tis time to leave," announced Jamie in a hushed tone.

"Just a few more moments," she whispered, drawing much closer.

When her fingers brushed across the rough bark, she encountered a piece of thread embedded in the tree. Goosebumps traveled up her arm and extended throughout her body.

"Do not remove it unless ye are prepared for the other path."

Ignoring the boy's words, Gwen tugged at the golden thread. The more she removed, the more she traveled around the ancient giant.

When she had almost completed her footpath around the tree, she yanked hard, snapping the thread free from its captor.

Gasping for breath, Gwen stumbled as her vision blurred and a great roaring filled her ears. And in a flash of brilliant lights, the ground beneath her opened, and she spiraled into an unknown abyss.

Chapter Five

"A thimble cannot protect a person from the sharp blade of truth." ~Wisdom of the Elder Weaver

Bitter cold seeped into Gwen's bones as she fought against the tide of inky blackness. Words refused to form in her mind to utter her discomfort and seek aid. Fear clutched at her with its sharp talons. Why couldn't she move? Open her eyes? Speak? Her heart beat rapidly against her chest. Doing her best to slow her erratic breathing, she waited for her body to make some attempt at movement. Minutes ticked by in agonizing torture until she was able to open one eye. White clouded her vision, along with more pain. Her hands dug into the ground and encountered freezing mush.

"Snow?" Her tone was garbled and barely coherent to her own ears.

With an indrawn hiss, Gwen managed to raise her painful body up to a sitting position and fully opened her eyes. She wrapped her arms around her knees and surveyed the snow-covered landscape through her hazy vision. Nothing seemed familiar. The autumn foliage, her horse, *and* Jamie had disappeared.

A whimper rose from her throat. *Do not panic, do not panic, do not panic!*

She lifted a shaky fist to her mouth to squelch the scream.

I must have hit my head, and this is all a nightmare.

Inspecting her head with her hands, Gwen found no injury. She glanced down at her body, trying to discern if there were any wounds from a fall. A glint of something lay matted against her coat. Removing the wet mass, she lifted it out in front of her.

"Thread?" Confused and frightened, Gwen stuffed the bunched up thread into the pocket of her coat.

Some of her memories flitted back into her mind as she tried to distinguish those from what she was witnessing. Gone was everything she knew. She didn't even think to bring her cell phone on their trek across the hilly terrain.

And where are you, Jamie? Were you injured?

Tears stung her eyes, but she quickly blinked them back. Survivor instincts took over. She had to find him. Though her jacket was fur-lined, it would not be adequate apparel in these harsh elements. Granted it was only a light dusting of snow, Gwen had no idea when more would descend.

Regardless of her situation, she had to make her way to shelter or find some help.

Gwen stretched out her legs and rolled to the side. Dizziness continued to hamper her progress. Gritting her teeth, she crawled over to a fallen tree stump. After pulling herself on top, she swiped a hand across her nose.

Her teeth chattered, which was more from fear than the cold. As she took in her surroundings once more, Gwen judged it best to rest for five more minutes and then attempt the journey toward civilization.

Lifting her head, she uttered a silent prayer to her

guardian angels. *Please protect and guide me. Let me find help and Jamie.*

A falcon's screech startled her. Looking over her shoulder, Gwen watched its flight across the gray sky. It made sweeping circles before disappearing over the treetops.

"Have you sent me a friend to show me the way? Shall I go south? Is this your message, angels?"

She swallowed and made to stand. Biting her lip, Gwen waited for the onslaught of pain or dizziness. When neither appeared, she smiled. Pulling the collar up around her neck, Gwen started forward slowly. With each step, her strength returned, along with hope.

No longer did she fear the path ahead. Anything was better than the alternative. Either she was truly demented or worse.

Am I dead?

But if it was the latter, how could she feel the bite of the wind? Was not Heaven a warm and beautiful place?

"I will *not* submit to this madness." She raised a fist to the sky. "I am descended from the great King Hywel. His blood and those of my ancestors' flow within me. From the first to the last, I am strong, and I *will* survive."

A burst of laughter bubbled forth from Gwen. She paused and shook her head. *If anyone heard your hysterical rant, they'd believe you hit your head.*

"Aye, King John would surely want to hear about this *great* King Hywel." A male voice shouted before striding forth from the trees.

The blood thundered in her ears as she took in the man's cold, harsh expression. The sickening stench of her own terror cloaked around her as he moved closer. Her stomach lurched while she pressed her fist to her chest.

The monster spat on the snow-covered landscape. "Can ye not speak?"

A scream lodged in Gwen's throat as she slumped to the ground.

****

"We are not alone," declared Andrew. He dismounted swiftly and knelt on one knee. After inspecting the ground, he nudged the horse dung with his fingers. "Not hard. Made after the snowfall."

Owain unsheathed his sword, scanning the area around them.

Patrick leaned forward on his horse. "Nearby?"

Standing, Andrew pointed through the dense trees. "Unsure. They traveled through here. Should we take another path?"

Uneasiness settled within Patrick like a lodestone. "There is none. If we took another road, it would merely hinder our journey to Urquhart."

"With the skirmishes happening throughout our land, do ye deem it wise to continue?" asked Owain.

Patrick slowly unsheathed his sword. "I have nae desire to come upon twenty armed men loyal to King John. The advantage would be to gather information and forward it to the MacKays. They can get a message to our king."

Letting out a soft curse, Owain nodded. "Now we are spies for King William. I would prefer a swift battle."

"We will proceed with caution." Patrick pointed to Andrew. "I shall lead, but I want ye to follow in the rear. Your eyes and skill with bow and arrow might be required."

The man gave a swift salute and quickly gathered his weapons from the side of his horse. Adjusting them securely over his shoulder, he then mounted his animal.

Patrick gave a curt nod to Owain in passing as he urged his horse along the path the others had previously taken. When the first snowflake landed on his face, he grimaced.

As he entered the darkness of the pine trees, Patrick slowed the pace of his horse. A trickling of unease crept up the back of his neck. Without warning, the hiss of an arrow narrowly missed his face. He bolted from his horse—sword arm ready for any attackers. A second arrow entered his shoulder with a sickening thud. Searing pain exploded down his left arm, and he fought the wave of dizziness. Keeping his grip on his sword, he dropped to the ground and crawled to the trunk of a nearby tree.

Owain was at his side instantly. "How bad?"

"Partially embedded. I need ye to cut off the shaft of the arrow."

Owain removed his dirk and cleanly sliced off most of the arrow.

Patrick stood. "Bastard is on the right. Go aid Andrew."

The man sneered. "Gladly."

Keeping his back against the giant tree, Patrick raised his sword arm in front of him. Fighting the wave of dizziness, he blinked several times. Blood trickled down his left arm, leaving dark splotches on the ground. Clenching his jaw, he did his best to seal off the pain and walked away from his protection. With cautious steps, he followed the movement of gruff voices until he came upon his own men.

Owain smacked the dead body with his sword. "Never had a chance to fight ye."

"Two of my arrows took him down without him uttering a complaint," boasted Andrew quietly.

"Others?" Patrick, blessed with a keen sight, kept his gaze outward.

"'Tis only the one. Must have been keeping watch," responded Andrew.

Patrick turned toward his men. "Then others will be here to replace him."

"Ye are wounded," stated Owain. "I should tend to the arrow."

"Nae," Patrick dismissed. "When we have—"

A blood chilling scream tore through the trees, halting any further conversation.

Placing a finger to his lips for the others to remain silent, Patrick motioned his guards to surround the enemy. He might be wounded, but nothing would prevent him from aiding whoever was in need.

As he stormed ahead, another scream ripped through the air. Coming to a partial clearing, Patrick barely made out the tiny figure of the lad. From his appearance, he wore odd clothing and shoes.

"Ye bitch! Your screams will go unheard. Ye will tell us the truth. Who is the king ye speak of?"

"Stop slapping me! And who are you?" she bit out in a commanding tone.

By the hounds of Cuchulainn. Not a lad, but a female.

Patrick looked to his left, confirming Owain's position, and then swept his gaze to the right for

Andrew's.

Three more men gathered around the apparent leader. From their lowly appearances, he judged they were not men loyal to King John. Unless, they fashioned themselves in this manner to travel under the guise of men living here.

Foolish and deadly.

The female's captor gripped her chin. "Ye speak in a strange tongue." He glanced over his shoulder at his men. "I believe King John will want to have words with this ugly wench. Despite her unseemly appearance, she can warm our beds on our journey.

Patrick straightened. *Traitors on our land.*

The female attempted to wrench free from her captor but could not break away from his hold.

"There is no one to hear your screams. *No one* to come to your aid. When we are finished with ye, ye will be begging to give us the answers we seek."

The men around her snickered in obvious satisfaction of either inflicting pain or slaking their pleasure with her body.

From his position, Patrick noted how the fear, stark and vivid glittered in those pale eyes. He'd witnessed this emotion many a time from others—as well as himself. His grip on his sword tightened, along with his fury. The pain in his shoulder diminished as his anger grew. Emerging from his hiding place, he moved across the clearing.

"Ye made a grave error in coming to the Great Glen. And another to think that *no one* would aid the lass." Patrick's voice as sharp as the deadly weapon he held.

The hiss of blades rent the air, but the traitors were

caught by surprise with the sudden appearance of Owain and Andrew. Within moments, Patrick's men had managed to take down all three.

Their leader shoved the lass to the ground, unsheathing his sword. "Will ye fight me? Or are ye too weak?"

Patrick advanced slowly. "Ye play a deadly game."

"Let me cleave his heart from his chest." Owain snarled, inching closer to the man.

Their foe took a step back. "'Tis not a fair fight. Three against my sword arm."

Patrick arched a brow. "Yet, ye were ready to take liberties with an unarmed lass."

"She speaks of another king," the man hissed out.

"And ye spoke of King John! Ye have nae right to be here." Patrick leveled his blade at the man. "Furthermore, I consider all men who force themselves on any woman to be vermin."

The man spat on the ground near the lass. Her look of disgust was evident as she scooted farther away from him.

"Soon, ye and your kind will know the wrath of King John. England shall rule over this desolate land. It is best ye die now."

Patrick let loose his fury. "Ye have trespassed on land that is not friendly to those who harbor ill will against any woman or man. Your thieving and harm against our people ends now." He gave a curt nod to his men. "This *enemy* is mine. Do not interfere."

Both men grumbled a curse.

Patrick's momentary glance at his men cost him. The man charged forward.

"*No!*"

The lass' shout proved to be a blessing, and Patrick veered sharply in time to miss a deadly blow to his chest. Taking the advantage, he lunged forward, and the battle of blades began in earnest. Both men were intent on either maiming the other or ending it with death's kiss.

Patrick's strength ebbed as the minutes dragged on between each swipe of their blades. His opponent was vastly skilled and more muscular. When he suffered a blow to the head, Patrick barely missed another one to his wounded shoulder. As his attacks became more violent, so did his breathing. With each strike of his blade, the pain intensified in his shoulder. Doing his best to ignore the agonizing burning, he focused on his foe's weakness. The man's bulk made it difficult to move swiftly, and Patrick prayed this would be his enemy's undoing.

The man continued to plague Patrick's left side, and any attempt to thwart his actions only increased the threat of losing. Blood now seeped into his eyes, causing his vision to blur. The fighting had to cease—now.

Today is not the day I die!

With a great roar, Patrick clutched his sword with both hands and lunged forward. His foe slipped on a soft patch of snow and gave Patrick the opening he needed. He cleaved his blade into the man's chest.

The man dropped his sword in stunned shock. Glancing down at his chest, he slurred a few jumbled words and fell to the ground.

Patrick's chest heaved with the exertion of the battle. Brushing a hand across his brow, he tried to wipe the blood away from his eyes. He winced when his fingers encountered the gash above his right brow. Stumbling to a fallen log, he sat down.

Owain ran to his side. "Thank the Goddess I didn't have to put a blade in one of the bastard's arms to stop this madness."

Patrick snorted. "Did ye not hear my order to *not* interfere?"

"As I recall, I made no oath."

"Your muttered curse was your vow to me." Patrick leaned forward against his sword and frowned. "Where is Andrew?"

Owain brushed a hand down the back of his neck. "We have a problem."

Patrick lowered his head. "So far, this journey has been fraught with too many. Do confess."

"Andrew is searching for the lass. She took advantage of the battle and ran off into the trees."

"By the hounds!" Patrick stood abruptly, ignoring the burning fire in his left shoulder. "And this is the thanks I get in return?" He waved his right hand dismissively outward. "Allow her to return to wherever she came from."

"She does not look like anyone from these parts. Do ye not deem it wiser we find out why she was traveling so deep in the glen without any guards or a maid? Her strange cloak and trews will not keep her from the harsh storm passing through here."

Blast the man! Owain's account was correct, and Patrick clenched his jaw. What possessed him to take this journey? "Which direction?"

"Heading south toward MacKay lands."

"Gather up their swords and horses," commanded Patrick, striding with intent after the lass.

"And the dead?"
"Leave their bodies for the wolves."

Chapter Six

"If the lion has become predatory, be wary ye do not become its prey." ~MacFhearguis Motto

Tree limbs smacked Gwen's face, their stinging blow barely missing her eyes as she darted through the thick forest. There was no time to consider if the wetness streaking down her cheeks was blood or tears. Her body screamed at her to rest, but her mind rebelled. Regardless of the burning in her lungs from the exertion of running, she had to put some distance between her and the madness she'd left behind. Tears blurred her vision upon recalling the images of the earlier battle of swords.

Do not dwell on it. Keep pushing onward. I must reach help and escape this insanity of a nightmare.

A deer, startled by her flight, darted out from its enclosure, and she almost collided with the animal. Instead, she tripped over a tree root and tumbled across the forest floor. Gasping for air, she spat out dead leaves and slush.

The world spun as Gwen attempted to right her body into a sitting position.

"Bloody hell," she hissed, more from fear than taking a spill. Glancing in all directions, she let her racing heart settle. Trying to discern any hint of noise, Gwen kept her senses alert and used this short time to gather her wits.

Stretching out her legs, she took a swift inspection of her body. No breaks in her limbs, but she knew there would be bruises later. After gently touching her face, she held out her hands in front of her. Blood stained her fingers from the apparent scratches embedded into the soft flesh. In addition, her blouse was torn and frayed along the bottom.

Frightened, weary, and utterly confused, Gwen swallowed the lump of despair lodged in her throat. She was never one prone to hysterics, even if this appeared to warrant the first time ever weeping fit.

Gwen lifted her gaze to a single shaft of sunlight streaming through the dense forest. It fell on the ground next to her, along with the dusting of snowflakes. Gingerly, she stretched out her fingers, allowing the light and warmth to infuse her spirit. Not one given to praying, she felt the time had come in her life. Was it desperation that leads a person to a humble prayer? Would God or a Goddess hear her words?

After the death of her parents at a young age and being fostered with various families most of her life, none had showed her the basics of any religion. With so many questions, she sought out her answers among the local churches and wise women who dwelled in the hills. Each one told her the same. She had to follow her heart to find peace. And so, she disregarded them, believing one day she might call upon them and took no comfort in any belief.

Her lips trembled. "If anyone can hear me, please send help. If I'm dying, then I pray…" She swallowed, trying to banish the fear. "I *pray* I have brought no harm to another. I've tried to be a good person."

Gwen brought her knees to her chest and lowered her head. "Please, *please* send help."

"Are ye injured, lass?"

The deep male voice startled Gwen. His question was one filled with concern as she slowly lifted her head. The air stilled around her. Eyes which mirrored the green hills near her home held her captive in their power. She recognized him as the one who fought her first captor. The warrior stood tall, extremely so, and his shoulders spanned the length of a large tree trunk. She took in the dark auburn hair curling around his face, and a small shaft of sunlight peeking through the trees, highlighted the golden streaks in his hair.

"Savior or Demon?" she asked in a hushed tone, too weak to run away.

The man frowned. "Neither."

Fear replaced curiosity. "Oh, God, you've sent the devil to take my soul. I must have wronged another."

The giant rubbed a hand vigorously over his face. "By the hounds, are ye not right in the head?" Irritation laced his words as he made to reach for her.

Her eyes widened in alarm. In an attempt to scoot away from his aid, Gwen's back slammed into a tree.

He fisted his hands on his hips. Words spewed forth from him, and she fought to understand the meaning. Was it Gaelic? Again, she felt her head for any signs of trauma or lumps. She pondered the idea she might have fallen at the yew tree. Her memory was too murky to recall anything significant.

Biting her lower lip, she stood slowly, keeping her back against the tree for support. The man raked a hand through his hair while he continued with his rant. As if coming out of a trance, Gwen noticed a stick protruding from his left shoulder. Blood oozed from the wound and traveled down his arm and chest, as well as a nasty cut above his brow.

"You're the one injured," she blurted out. "I only have a few scratches and bruises."

His ranting ceased, and he stared at her in obvious confusion.

Gwen moved away from the tree. "Your arm and the cut above your eye require medical treatment. Is there a hospital nearby in this God forsaken place?"

The giant swept his gaze to his shoulder and then returned his attention to her. "Aye, 'tis wounded I am, but I do not ken your other words."

Gwen almost laughed at the irony. "Good. That makes two of us, because I'm having a difficult time *understanding* why you're oblivious to your wound." If she could convince him to seek medical assistance, perhaps she'd be able to find her way back to Leòmhann.

She took another step toward him. Taking in his odd appearance and clothing, including the sword by his side, she didn't think he had anything clean to staunch the blood flow. Obviously, Gwen was not about to relinquish her coat. Reaching for the torn material on her blouse, she ripped a good portion free. Her clothing might have some smudges and dirt, but she'd bet her last coin that hers was cleaner.

She ignored his indrawn breath and bunched up the material. "Until we can get you to a hospital, I'm going to apply pressure around the wound. I can strip some more of the fabric and wrap it around your arm to keep the pressure."

The man stiffened when she wrapped the material

around the protruding object in his shoulder, yet not a word of objection passed from his lips. "Can you hold it here?"

He swiftly complied, and Gwen tore more of her blouse free, exposing a portion of her stomach.

"Sweet Mother Danu," he hissed.

She lifted her head, noting his stunned expression. "If you're offended, then look the other way." Goodness, the man must think her hideous and fat. Gwen gritted her teeth, doing her best to temper her hurt and anger. "Can you lift your left arm a little? I'm going to wrap it a second time."

Refusing to meet his gaze, Gwen waited patiently. When he slowly lifted his arm, she wrapped the swatch of cloth around and under his arm. Securing it gently, she took a step back. After wiping her nose with the back of her hand, she grimaced at the sight of blood staining her fingers.

As she started forward, a large hand clamped on her shoulder, staying her movements. "Nae."

She gave him a disbelieving look over her shoulder. "No *what*?"

"Do not flee."

"Bastard," she uttered softly, instantly regretting the barb.

His green eyes darkened to shards of emeralds. Yet, she no longer feared the giant. The weariness of her situation overrode polite conversation. "All I wanted to do was clean my hands in the snow pile near the trees. It's much cleaner than the muddy mush near us."

He slowly released his hold on her.

Gwen made quick strides to the tree and did her

best to get rid of the blood stains. When she turned around, the giant stood mere inches from her. "What now?"

"Why are ye traveling without any guards? Where is your kin?"

She blanched at the remark. "Has your injury caused you to have hallucinations?" *And here I thought I was the one.* Though she was curious as to how he got the wound.

"Answer my question," he demanded, glaring at her.

Narrowing her eyes at him, she dared to poke him in his broad chest. "Why would I require guards? And my *kin* is none of your concern."

A flurry of activity swarmed around them as two men emerged forth from the trees.

"Thank the Gods and Goddesses," proclaimed one of the men. "Ye found the lass, Patrick. Did ye ask her why she is traveling in these parts? Where is her kin?"

Gwen let out a frustrated sigh, recognizing both men as companions of this giant they called Patrick. "For the love of angels, what is wrong with you both?" She waved a hand about. "Why the interest in my family?"

"Strange tongue and clothing," announced the third man, rubbing a hand over his chin. "Has she told ye why she is without her kin? Why is she dressed in this manner, and what did they do to her hair? Perchance an outcast?"

With a groan, Gwen pushed past the giant and proceeded to walk away. She quickly zipped up her jacket. "I've definitely hit my head. Or maybe this is some bizarre delusion. Must find my way back to

Leòmhann."

"*Leòmhann?*" echoed Patrick.

Gwen paused and turned around slowly. Hope flared like a beacon in her dark and confusing world. "Do you know the way?"

Wariness reflected in Patrick's features. "Aye."

"Wonderful! If you could take me back there, I'm sure someone can drive you to the hospital to treat your wound."

He lifted his sword. With her heart pounding fiercely, Gwen took in his massive muscles, most likely trained to wield a blade with deadly force. Would he take aim at her defenseless position? And why were any of these men roaming the forest with weapons, dressed in medieval garb, *and* riding horses? Was it a historical reenactment gone horrifically wrong?

Dear angels, I asked for help. Not this nightmare.

Gwen swallowed and met his hard glare. "I am a guest there. Might I ask why you are dressed in this fashion? Seems peculiar to me."

One of the men tapped Patrick on the arm. "I reckon she's taken a tumble and landed on her head."

Patrick ignored the other man. "Currently, Leòmhann has nae female guests."

Appalled by his statement, she countered, "I disagree. Perhaps you've not been made aware of my arrival. Regardless, I'm not going to debate semantics. I thank you for rescuing me, but I must return to Leòmhann. And you must get yourself to a hospital."

"Do ye understand what the lass is saying?" asked the other man, scratching the side of his face.

This debate over her words was giving Gwen a pounding headache. "Will you kindly show me the way back to Leòmhann?"

"Nae," replied Patrick, tersely.

Refusing to argue any further with the demented man, Gwen dismissed him with a wave of her hand and stormed away. "You're a bastard," she muttered.

She had only taken a few steps when rough hands halted her progress once again. Patrick abruptly turned her around. Anger burned within the depths of his green eyes, but she refused to cower in front of this man. Her energy was depleted, and all she wanted to do was go back to Leòmhann. Was it too much to ask?

"Even if I wanted to, snowfall hampers the path back to Leòmhann. 'Tis more than two days' ride *without* the harsh weather."

Crestfallen, Gwen blew out an irritated breath and lowered her head. *How did I get so far away from the castle?*

Patrick gripped her chin, forcing her to meet his gaze. "I am not a bastard. I was born after wedlock."

Confusion battled within Gwen. The man was far too close. Too domineering. Too male.

She should fear him, not get lost in his features. Snow dusted his hair, and she longed to brush the moisture away. Blinking several times, she focused on what he said to her. "I am sorry for cursing at you. I'm normally not prone to swearing."

He released his hold on her, yet made no move to back away. "Ye will be safe in our company."

"Then if I can't return to Leòmhann, can you take me to the local police station?"

A frown creased his brow. "I do not ken this place. Ye will travel with us to Urquhart."

"Urquhart?" she squeaked. "But what about those

men back there? Should we not report this incident? They could be doing harm to others."

"Do not fear. They are all dead."

Her eyes grew wide, and her breathing became labored. "*Dead*?"

"Aye. I deem they would have done grave harm to ye. They and King John have plagued our lands for many moons."

Gwen required space to breathe. Lights danced in an arc around them. These men were clearly demented. What was she thinking? If she went willingly with them, who knows what they'd do to her. They spoke about a king long dead as if he was still alive, and they battled with archaic weapons.

She shoved at his massive chest. "Move away."

When he didn't comply, she ducked under his arm and made to flee. He reached out and grasped her hand. "I will not harm ye. I give ye my word."

"Really? But you just told me you *killed* those men. Could you not have rendered them unconscious? Tied them up and deliver them to the authorities? What kind of lunatic goes around wielding a sword and taking the life of another?" She took in huge gulps of cold air, trying not to scream.

"Did they hit ye on the head, lass?" asked one of the other men.

Again, Gwen tried to determine if she'd been knocked out at some point in this mad world she'd tumbled into. Her body did ache, but her head appeared to be fine, except for the pain behind her eyes. "I need a drink and an aspirin," she mumbled.

Patrick turned toward his men, keeping his grip on her. "Owain, fetch my horse. Andrew, tether the other horses together. Ye will be in charge of seeing to them until we reach Urquhart Castle."

Her shoulders sagged in resignation. "So how far is Urquhart?"

"Since we have lost valuable daylight, we won't be there until tomorrow."

"And we're traveling by horses?" she asked, her voice unsteady.

"Unless ye prefer to walk, aye."

Gwen remained silent as the one called Owain brought forth a large horse. Black as night the animal trotted forward.

"Ye should let me tend to the arrow first," the man remarked, handing the reins to Patrick.

"When we find shelter for the night."

Clearly I've lost my mind. Blades and arrows? Gwen looked past the man. "Where's my horse?"

Patrick mounted his animal and gestured to Owain. "Raise the lass up here."

"I reckon she can ride with me or Andrew. Ye are wounded."

"Excuse me. I can ride a horse." Irritation sparked her words.

"Nae," bit out Patrick.

Owain moved toward her. "Give me your foot, lass."

Gwen folded her arms over her chest. "I can ride my own horse!"

Patrick's fierce growl might scare his men, but Gwen was beyond caring about anything. She glared up at him. When he leaned forward, she refused to budge. "If ye do not comply, I will have Owain strap your body across my horse."

"Fine," she snapped, lifting her foot for Owain. "But don't blame me if I happen to slam against your injured arm."

A wicked smile curved his features as Patrick straightened in the saddle. "Your tongue is as sharp as my blade, lass."

She snorted at the insult.

When Gwen settled herself in front of the man, her body went rigid. Patrick had dared to put his wounded arm around her waist. His breath was hot against her cheek. "Try not to slam too hard."

Her face heated at the remark, and she couldn't fathom why.

Chapter Seven

"If ye are unsure of which colors to grace your canvas, take a walk among the trees." ~Wisdom of the Elder Weaver

Never before had Patrick wanted to throttle a woman.

Her endless chatter and arguing with him made his head spin. Unable to discern some of the words she spewed forth only infuriated him more. And what possessed the blasted female to wear such tight-fitting trews? Did she know what view she presented to him? Or to the others? Thank the Gods she fastened her cloak, if ye could call it such. She must have stolen the garment from a child.

When she ripped apart her chemise, exposing part of her skin, the lustful beast in him roared. Embarrassed by his lack of control, he'd turned to anger.

"I don't understand how quickly the weather has shifted?" she protested. "It was a glorious autumn morning."

Patrick tried not to roll his eyes. Instead, he blew out an exaggerated breath, and the frosty air mingled around them.

"How severe is the pain?" she asked, glancing over her shoulder and giving him a concerned expression.

Her rosy cheeks and full lips tempted him to do

things he had forsaken many moons ago.

"Are you going to pass out?"

"Why would I do so?" he asked quietly.

"You haven't spoken a word since we've started this trek to Urquhart. If you have noticed, I'm doing all the talking. Often times, when someone is in extreme pain, they can faint or keep silent to block the agony. Which one are you attempting?"

The lass sat too near, smelling like the woods on a spring day—wild and fresh. "As a trained warrior, we learn to silence the pain." *Unlike the need to steal a kiss.*

Her brow furrowed. "Interesting. You are all taking this reenactment far too seriously."

And there again were those words he was unable to fathom. He shook his head and let his gaze rest on the landscape below.

Thankfully, she resumed her position and kept silent.

By the time they reached Urquhart land, shards of pain seared from his shoulder to his hand. Though snow dusted them both, beads of sweat had broken out along his brow. If they could reach the cave Alastair MacKay mentioned to him last year, he'd have Owain remove the arrow shaft and mend the wound.

Patrick brought his horse to a halt. Gesturing for Owain, he waited for the man to approach. "Ride southwest through the grove. I believe there is a cave tucked in the back of the mountain we descended from. When you come to an ash tree, there will be a druid's mark. If so, return and we shall spend the night there."

The man gave him a curt nod and took off.

His companion chose to turn part way, giving him

a muddled look. "Why are we not staying in a hotel?"

"I do not ken your meaning," he replied gruffly.

"Inn? Comfortable Bed and Breakfast or even a castle might be nice. Are we really going to have to make camp in a cave?"

Between fighting the pain and not being able to understand some of the woman's words, Patrick judged it best to ignore her.

Her restless movements and mumblings tried his patience. Clenching his jaw, Patrick tried to steady his horse. The animal sensed the irritation from both his master and the woman who continued to babble on.

"Will ye cease your complaints," he snapped, then regretted the harshness of his tone.

Her back went rigid. "I don't recall *complaining* about anything. I'm trying to understand why we can't find indoor accommodations. Is it too much for you to answer my question?"

Patrick wiped a hand across his brow. *Hurry, Owain, before I toss the lass off my horse.*

"What bothers ye, lass?" asked Andrew, coming alongside them.

Patrick gave a warning look to the man, but Andrew chose to ignore him.

"Can someone explain to me why we are spending the night outdoors? Isn't there a hotel or inn nearby?"

Andrew frowned in obvious confusion.

Patrick smirked. *'Tis good to know I am not the only one confounded by her words*

"There is nothing between us and Urquhart, lass. Shelter for ye is our concern, aye. Do not fret. I ken Owain is searching for a fitting area."

The lass surprised them both by reaching out and

placing a gentle hand on Andrew's arm. "Thank you for giving me an answer. It's really all I wanted."

Andrew beamed, appearing to sit straighter on his horse.

And Patrick let out a groan.

"Are ye going to pass out?" asked Andrew, returning his attention to him.

"I think he's on the verge. I did ask him earlier, since he's been so quiet," added the lass. "Should I ride another horse?"

"Nae!" responded Patrick, heaving a sigh of relief as he spotted Owain galloping through the trees.

Andrew leaned near him. Mirth teased across his features. "Nae, ye are not going to pass out *or* nae to the lass' demands?"

Patrick ignored him and waited for Owain. The man smiled. "Aye. There is a cave like ye spoke of. Enough room for all of us."

"Lovely. I'm spending the night in a cave with three men whom I've never met."

Patrick leaned forward, the effort inflicting more pain within his body. "Do not forget these men did save your life."

Her mouth opened on a sharp indrawn breath and then snapped shut.

"Lead onward," ordered Patrick.

Swiftly they all followed the man's lead through the grove of trees. Passing the ash tree Alastair MacKay had mentioned, Patrick noted the mark of one particular druid and smiled. Cathal was a good friend here in these parts of the land. The path dipped and curved, leading them to the back of the mountain. As Patrick slowed his horse, he scanned the area for a possible cave.

Owain dismounted and pointed to a thick group of pine trees. "'Tis hidden behind. Ye will have to bend low to enter."

"How were ye able to come upon the entrance?" asked Patrick, bringing his horse to a halt.

The man chuckled. "Kept searching until a wee beastie came scampering forth."

"Beastie?" The lass bent forward, examining the ground.

"Do not worry. 'Tis merely a lone hare," reassured Owain.

Her resulting movement sent a fire of pain through his left side. Patrick clenched his jaw so tight he feared it might snap. "Will someone remove the lass from my horse," he bit out tersely.

She gave him a horrified expression. "I'm so sorry. I forgot about your arm."

He closed his eyes, waiting for the pain to lessen. After the lass dismounted, Patrick opened his eyes. Slowly, he did the same, but leaned against the animal for two breaths.

Owain came to his side. "Go inside. I shall find some brush and dead limbs to start a fire."

"And leave me alone with the lass?" He snorted, giving a firm pat to the animal. "Nae. See that she is secure, and I will gather the wood. Her constant drivel has left me with a headache."

They both turned at the sound of her gasp. Hurt shone in those pale blue eyes, and Patrick instantly lamented the cutting remark. She turned away from their gazes, her shoulders trembling. Unwilling to offer an apology, Patrick clenched his hands and stormed away.

Passing Andrew along the path, he ignored the man when he started to speak. Never in all his years had he behaved so poorly toward a female. What was it about the lass that had him spouting rude and bitter words? He raked a hand through his hair as his steps led him toward an ash tree.

Brushing his fingers over the druid's mark, he sighed heavily. "I require your counsel, Cathal. Am I to go mad like my brother, Michael?"

Snow continued to drift around him. Birds flitted along the limbs of the tree, their silence an omen of the weather shifting. Soon the land would be covered with snow, and Patrick closed the door on his angst and went in search of kindling and wood for a fire.

Upon returning to the cave, he dumped what he had collected in the middle. The lass sat huddled in a corner, never meeting his gaze. Andrew positioned himself at the entrance, and Owain went to work on starting the fire.

Ashamed by his earlier actions, Patrick drew near the lass. "Forgive my outburst of harsh words."

She fidgeted with the bottom of her cloak. "I pray your headache has dissipated."

Her tone betrayed her outward appearance, and Patrick heard the censure in her voice. *Ye are a brave little bird.* Stooping down next to her, he dared to touch her chin, forcing her to meet his gaze. She darted him a surprised look. "My actions are a result of my wound."

"Or ye are with fever," interjected Owain.

He lowered his head. "A possibility."

The lass grasped his hand, hers warm and soft. "Then we must cleanse it immediately."

Now it was Patrick's turn to be surprised. "Are ye a healer?"

She snickered. "Of injuries left by an arrow? Certainly not. But I've had medical training and CPR at university."

Unable to fathom the meaning of some of her words, Patrick simply nodded. He stood, bringing her with him, refusing to let go of her tiny hand. "Ye have not shared your name with us."

Red blotches immediately appeared on her cheeks.

Patrick released her hand. "I am called Patrick. My guards are known as Owain, who is tending to the fire, and by the entrance is Andrew."

"Guards? Impressive. Are you someone important or related to royalty?"

Patrick burst out in laughter, along with his other men. Seeing her confused expression, he explained, "Nae, not royalty. But I am the brother to the Laird."

"Interesting. Must be an important *laird*," she admitted.

"Verra," added Owain. "If ye are skilled in any healing, I shall welcome your aid."

The lass smiled and thrust out her hand. "I'll do what I can to assist. I'm Gwen. Gwen Hywel."

Owain's eyes widened. "Truly?"

Her laughter surrounded Patrick in a musical web. But he was curious why she extended her arm outward.

Gwen's head bobbed with mirth as she lowered her hand. "Last I checked, that was my name."

"Owain's kin are Hywels'," declared Patrick, his curiosity now growing.

Gwen pressed a hand to her chest. "We could be related? Or share a common name. Supposedly, I am descended from the great King Hywel."

Patrick glanced at his friend. "Can ye state the same, Owain?"

"Aye," responded the man slowly. He moved toward her, taking her hand. "'Tis an honor to meet another from my land."

"Owain came into the service of my brother at a young age," remarked Patrick.

"Fascinating. You must share more later," suggested Gwen, giving the man a glorious smile. "I think it's wise we get to work on cleaning the wound on Patrick's shoulder."

"Agreed." Owain gestured Gwen away from her corner and to the fire. "Patrick, go sit against the wall. Ye did say the arrow did not pierce through to the other side, aye?"

"Ye are correct." Reaching the wall, Patrick slumped down against the cool stone. Fatigue settled around him.

Owain returned to his side with a satchel. Removing his dirk, he lifted the blade in front of Gwen. "Place the steel into the fire," he ordered.

She took the blade hesitantly. "For what purpose?"

"To seal the wound." Owain removed the bandages and gently lifted Patrick's cloak over the protruding stick. "The thick garment might have hindered its progress."

"No! That's barbaric. He requires stitches and antibiotics." She continued with her protests but complied and placed the dirk within the fire.

"Her words make nae sense," muttered Owain as he inspected the shoulder.

"Aye." Patrick leaned his head against the wall. "If

she is from your land, why does she spout in a strange tongue?"

His friend tapped a finger to his head. "By her odd clothing and speech, she might have been cast out of her clan." With deft fingers, Owain ripped the material free from around the afflicted area.

Gwen approached by their side. "Do you have anything I can use to boil water? We should clean the open wounds after you take the stick out."

"'Tis an arrow," countered Patrick.

She fisted her hands on her hips. "Regardless, we need clean water."

Owain pointed to his satchel. "Hand me the wine skin."

"Sweet angels. What world have I descended into?" Gwen crouched down beside Patrick, peering into the bag. Retrieving the wine skin, she held it up for inspection. "This is beautiful."

Patrick tapped a finger to his head, indicating their earlier conversation regarding the lass.

Owain fought to contain a smile forming on his mouth. Taking the wine skin, he poured a small amount over the wound and then handed it to Patrick. "Drink heavily."

Taking the skin, Patrick guzzled deeply. After he returned it to Gwen, he wiped his mouth with the back of his hand. "I am ready. Get this out of me."

Owain reached for his satchel and pulled forth a pouch. Producing a small item, he unraveled the material around the tool.

"Please tell me you're not going to *dig* it out of him?" The color had drained from Gwen's face, leaving her features ashen.

"Are ye going to question everything I do, lass?" protested Owain. "'Tis an arrow spoon to help remove the steel barb at the tip. Without it, the barb might have to be ripped out, tearing more within."

She swallowed. "Oh. Obviously, you have done this type of procedure before."

Owain returned his focus on Patrick's shoulder. "I cannot go swiftly. Do ye want something to bite down on?"

Patrick snickered, the wine already dulling his senses. "Make sure ye remove the entire bloody piece."

Owain's skillful fingers took hold of the protruding arrow. With his other hand, he eased the spoon underneath. Hot, burning pain shot through Patrick's shoulder. Clenching his right hand, he attempted to keep his breathing steady and his body still. While he closed his eyes, Patrick tried to banish the anguish.

Minutes ticked by in agonizing torture. Thank the Goddess, even the lass remained silent. The fire hissed and snapped in their small enclosure, echoing his mood. Waves after waves of pain washed over Patrick while his guard worked to dislodge the barb. Bile rose from his stomach, yet he refused to give it free rein. Tremors began to shake his body as he fought to control the blinding agony.

"Nasty bit of steel," announced Owain in victory.

Opening his eyes, Patrick glared at the offensive arrow barb.

The lass moved to his side and lifted the wine skin to his lips. He drank a few sips, but then drew back. "Thank ye."

Owain tossed the disgusting piece into the flames. He removed several smaller pouches from his satchel.

"I am going to place some healing herbs inside and then close it. Fetch me the blade, lass."

"Can you not wait until we reach Urquhart tomorrow? Maybe they can have someone send for a doctor to stitch the wound." Her question appearing taut with strain.

Patrick shook his head, too weary to argue with her.

"We have nothing to staunch the bleeding on the journey," confirmed Owain.

Quietly, Gwen went and retrieved the blade from the fire. The red-hot steel glowed like the eyes of a monster as she handed it to Owain.

The man waited for half a breath before leveling the flat end of the blade against his wound.

Patrick's vision blurred, the pain slamming into his entire body. He battled the blackness descending over him, luring him to an abyss. He refused to yield, clenching his jaw against the unbearable torment.

Cool fingers brushed against his brow. "It's over."

Her soothing words of comfort eased the torment of pain. Once again, she lifted the wine skin to his lips. Patrick longed to reach out and tug at one of her curls. Light from the fire danced off her hair, creating a magical effect.

Her luminous eyes scanned his features. "You're the bravest warrior I've ever encountered." After placing the wine skin by his side, she stood and went to the entrance of the cave.

Patrick's gaze followed her retreating form, noting the trembling of her limbs and unsteady steps.

Andrew made to stand. A look of concern brushed over his friend's face as he took her elbow, leading her out of the cave.

Something primal rose within Patrick. It clawed at him to strike out at the guard. No other man should dare touch the lass, save one.

Gwen belonged to him.

Chapter Eight

"When your heart is plagued with uncertainty, remove the offending emotion with your blade."
~MacFhearguis Motto

Sleep did not come easily. Between fits of horrific nightmares and echoes of battles, Gwen finally gave up on finding any blissful rest. She shifted on the hard ground, coming to a sitting position. Her entire body ached. Rubbing a hand over her forehead, she tried to ease the tension of her headache.

Glancing across the fire, she found Patrick in a rigid position with his head leaning against the back of the cavern's wall. His features did not appear to be strained, and she prayed he had found some rest.

After her declaration to Patrick, Gwen emptied what little she had in her stomach onto the ground outside the cave. She didn't even have the courage to send the man called Andrew away. He held her as she continued to retch over the fresh fallen snow. Never before had she witnessed such a horrific ordeal. Combined with what had happened to her earlier—fighting with those horrible men—the day had caught up with her body.

Nevertheless, Gwen's mind was another matter entirely. Her thoughts circled with all the pieces of this illogical world she found herself in. She prayed they would snap into place, and she would awake from this twisted nightmare.

Surely, it had to be. Nothing made sense. Men did not roam the highlands with swords and arrows on horseback, appearing straight from a different time period. Their speech and mannerisms were not what you would call modern.

When they reached Urquhart Castle, she firmly believed and prayed all would return to normal. She'd call Meggie or Adam to come rescue her from this situation. Her stomach clenched, recalling Jamie's words drifting through her memories.

"Do not remove it unless ye are prepared for the other path."

"Remove what?" she whispered, expecting the boy to answer.

She continued to sift through fragments of her memory, doing her best to put them in a cohesive order. The effort cost her more pain, and she blew out a frustrated breath. Getting slowly to her feet, Gwen stretched and proceeded to walk out of the cave.

Andrew stood abruptly. "Are ye going to be unwell again?"

Embarrassed, she shook her head and stepped outside into a landscape covered in white. She rubbed her hands together, taking in the crisp, cold air. The first etches of rose danced over the treetops, signaling the beginning of a new day.

Andrew draped his cloak over her shoulders. "'Tis a beautiful morn." He retreated for a moment. Swiftly returning to her side, he stated, "Here, eat this bannock and drink. Ye need to break your fast." He shoved the items into her hands.

Startled by his kindness, she murmured her thanks and took the biscuit and skin, praying it was not wine. Sniffing the contents, she almost smiled inwardly at finding the liquid merely water.

"Ye were strong last night, lass."

Gwen disagreed. "I did nothing but watch in stunned horror, and then I threw up." She nibbled on the hard food.

"Nae," said Andrew slowly. "Ye cared for Patrick and aided Owain. Removing a barb from flesh is nae easy to witness." Taking an arrow from his quiver, he held it outward. "This can be friend or foe."

Curious, she asked, "Did you make this?"

Smiling, he brushed his fingers over the wood. "Aye. From an ash tree. Spotted several limbs and asked Lugh and the Goddess for permission to remove them from her tree."

And now I can add pagan to the list of oddities. "Why Lugh?"

The man lifted the arrow to the morning light. "Are ye not familiar with the Sun God Lugh?"

"No. Tell me more," she encouraged between bites of her food.

"Legends say that the mighty Lugh never went into any battle without his magical spear made of ash. Furthermore, many bards have told the tale of Lugh of the Long Arm, suggesting the spear was a part of him. With each new arrow I fashion from an ash tree, I honor him. I pray over each after they are completed, so when I come into combat, my aim is true."

Gwen angled her head, watching as the dawn's first sliver of light touched the newly made arrow. "Friend *and* foe."

Andrew let out a sigh while lowering his arm. "Aye, lass."

"Gather your supplies. We are leaving," announced Patrick in a brusque tone.

Turning sharply, Gwen noted the scowl across the man's features as he directed his gaze on Andrew.

Quickly going to his side, she brushed her hand over his shoulder. Patrick flinched from her touch. "Please forgive me. I meant only to inquire and shouldn't have touched you. Are you in a lot of pain?"

"Tolerable."

Andrew stepped by his side. "The lass should ride with me."

"Did I not state to gather your supplies?" Patrick shifted his stance. "Gwen can share my horse."

Arching a brow at him, Andrew kept silent and proceeded to pack up his working tools.

"Why are you so stubborn, Patrick?"

His eyes widened. "I did not ken that protecting ye accounted for being stubborn."

"So you don't trust your men to protect me?"

He took a step near her, his presence surrounding her. Lifting his hand, his finger brushed away a curl from her cheek. This time it was Gwen who flinched. "Until we reach Urquhart, ye are under *my* protection."

Protection? Did I ask for a knight in shining armor in my prayers? The man infuriated and fascinated her. "I once asked if you were my Savior or Demon. I'm beginning to believe the latter."

A muscle twitched in his jaw. "And I deem I confessed to neither."

"If ye are both done arguing, we can depart," suggested Andrew.

"Aye," agreed Owain, emerging forth from the cave.

Swiftly glancing away from Patrick's heated gaze, Gwen removed Andrew's cloak. Although the morning was brisk, heat coursed through her veins and she tempered the burning in her cheeks with her cool hands. What was it with this man? She was drawn to him like forlorn sheep to a shepherd.

He's a brute, nothing more.

After returning Andrew's cloak, Gwen waited for Patrick to get on his horse. Allowing Andrew to assist her onto the animal, she then settled back against the man. Keeping her focus on the landscape, she suggested, "If you put your arm around my waist, I'll cradle it in my arms. This will allow support for your injured shoulder."

Leaning near her face, he added, "First, take my cloak and wrap it around your body. The garments ye have on are not enough for the harsh weather we may encounter."

Gwen glanced back at him. He was so close she could make out the golden flecks in his green eyes. Perfect jewels, she thought. Yet, her gaze drifted lower to his full lips. An ache of desire shot through her, as did a yearning to cup his face and taste the man.

"I should be asking if ye are the one with a fever, lass," he uttered softly.

The burr of his voice caused her to tremble. "Why?"

He brushed a finger over her cheek. "Your stain here reminds me of strawberries on a summer morn."

She blinked, feeling totally foolish, and turned away. Gaping at the man like a schoolgirl. What was wrong with her? Quickly gathering the material of his cloak, Gwen wrapped it around her. Again, his heat invaded into her skin, prickling in places she didn't understand.

It was useless trying to calm her racing pulse. "Put your arm around my waist."

When he complied, Gwen almost swooned. Why was this time different than the first time he held her? *You almost kissed the man!* Baffled by her own feelings and too many questions, she banished them all and cradled his arm within hers.

With the first lurch forward, Gwen felt him stiffen. He might be a strong warrior, but she reasoned the man could not deny his pain.

The scenery of the landscape blurred as more snow carpeted the land and trees. In trying to maintain a firm hold on Patrick's arm, she found her body had become rigid. After several hours on horseback, pain settled uncomfortably in her lower back and legs. Unaccustomed to riding with another on a horse, Gwen had forgotten the basics of riding, and she never found a relaxing rhythm. In truth, her last memorable ride on a horse had been two years ago. A birthday gift to herself—alone amongst the hills of Wales on a glorious summer day.

Your body is horribly out of shape.

When another hour bled into the next, Gwen began to clench her jaw. Closing her eyes, she attempted to will away the pain. If a trained warrior with a wounded shoulder could maintain his fortitude, surely she would be able to manage the horseback ride to Urquhart.

"How much farther?" she inquired, shifting slightly in an effort to alleviate the agony.

Patrick brought the animal to a halt. "Owain, help the lass down."

"Are we nearby?" She wanted to weep for joy, allowing the man to assist her from Patrick's horse.

"Nae." Patrick dismounted. He motioned her to the trees.

Confused, she followed on unsteady limbs. The man pushed aside the limbs heavy with snow, permitting her to go on through. After taking the lead, Patrick kept on walking forward.

"Where are we going?"

Silence greeted her while her steps slowed. Patrick parted more tree branches and pointed. When she peered around him, the view of the water sparkled even in the gray light of day. Snow fell gently over the landscape, giving her a picturesque view of the highlands. Her breath caught as she took in the beauty of the stark region, coupled with snowfall.

"Loch Ness," he confirmed.

"And Urquhart?"

"North."

Disappointment doused her earlier joy. "Do you think we'll reach the castle by nightfall?"

"Perchance sooner."

"Then side trips like this one will hamper our arrival." Pushing away from the tree, Gwen winced.

"Where is the pain?"

"It's *tolerable*." She refused to appear weak, returning the same remark he had shared with her earlier.

Patrick reached for her hand. His warmth and strength seeped through her skin. "Place both your hands against the bark with your feet some distance apart."

"And why am I doing this?"

The beginning of a smile tipped the corners of his mouth. "Trust me, lass. Ye are in pain from riding stiffly for many hours."

For reasons she couldn't fathom, Gwen had faith in the man. Removing her hand from his, she did as he instructed.

His presence loomed from behind her. "If ye will permit me, I shall roll my knuckles along your back."

Heat flared instantly up her neck, but Gwen nodded, giving him permission.

When the first contact of his fist swept across her back, Gwen let out a moan. Pain and pleasure fought for dominance. She closed her eyes against the sensations of his healing and seductive touch, allowing her body to ease from its rigid position.

"Let your limbs relax," he urged softly.

"Feels so good," she mumbled.

He splayed his fingers and massaged the knots along the column of her neck. Delicious pinpricks trickled down her back, along with the melting snow on her head. Gwen knew she presented a wretched sight, but she gave no care. His fingers caressed the top of her spine and wove their way down to both shoulders. By the time he finished, her body was on fire with another type of ache, but her muscles had loosened up. There was no denying the man ignited a spark within her.

Gwen turned around slowly.

He placed his hand above her on the tree, trapping her against the rough bark with his body. Lowering his head near her ear, he whispered, "Better?"

The word had her breathing rapidly. Gwen did the

unthinkable and pressed her cheek against him—his beard grazing her face. "Yes."

"Good." He breathed the word against her skin and withdrew.

He held her captive with the intensity of his gaze—compelling and magnetic. She had contained her inner woman within a cocoon for so long she yearned to be set free. If this was a distorted nightmare, she was determined to leave it on a positive experience.

When neither made a move to part, the butterfly emerged. Gwen lifted her hand and cupped his cheek. His eyes darkened as he turned his face into her palm, pressing his warm lips against her skin. A new and unexpected heat rushed inside her, and she gasped with the pleasure.

Patrick took a step back, breaking their connection. A slash of wind slapped across her face, cooling the heat of their encounter.

She smiled weakly. "Thank you."

The man dipped his head. "My pleasure." With a wave of his hand, he gestured outward for her to proceed.

As they emerged forth from the trees, Gwen avoided the stern expressions on Andrew and Owain's faces. She didn't require a mirror to know her face burned with the fire of passion. The heat extended to every pore across her skin. Who knew that a kiss within the palm could be so sensual? She flexed her hand, recapturing the moment as she waited for Patrick to get on his horse.

After help from Andrew, she settled back against Patrick and resumed her position of securing his arm within hers.

No more words were spoken on their trek to Urquhart. With the pain now manageable and her body relaxed, Gwen kept her focus on the land and the steady rhythm of the horse.

At least when she awoke, she'd recall this time when a Highlander enchanted her so much, and how she'd almost allowed the man to take possession of her body.

One sensuous kiss spoke volumes.

Absently, Gwen brought her fingers to her lips, imagining him touching her there.

Chapter Nine

"If ye take your focus away from the loom, be wary of the reason why." ~Wisdom of the Elder Weaver

Urquhart Castle's shadow loomed near the water's edge, and Patrick heaved an inner sigh of relief at seeing the home of the Dragon Knights. Thank the Gods his current companion remained quiet for the duration of their journey. His behavior back in the woods had gone from concern to lustful animal, with him aching to kiss more than the hand she presented to him.

Gwen beguiled and confounded him. A wee slip of a lass with a tongue as sharp as the sting of a nettle. She continued to lure him to her, snaring him with her beauty and body. Even now, Patrick's cock betrayed him, swelling uncomfortably while he recalled her bent position against the tree. Images of stripping those trews from her heart-shaped bottom had him in agony.

Lust, 'tis merely lust. Slake your need on another.

Disgust filled him. Patrick wanted only this female bouncing softly against him, not another.

Swiftly slamming the door on his thoughts, he maneuvered his horse near the bridge and came to a halt. Andrew and Owain appeared on either side.

"MacFhearguis! What brings ye out in such foul weather? Has your brother tossed ye out?" Angus

MacKay bellowed from the gate tower.

"And have ye nae men to watch your lands? Must the leader of the Dragon Knights take up a position to stand guard?" scoffed Patrick.

The man braced his hands on the ledge of the tower. "As all leaders should."

The grating of steel signified the opening of the portcullis, and Angus waved him onward.

"What are Dragon Knights?" asked Gwen, adding, "And why is everyone dressed in these medieval garments?"

"Good friends." Confused by her second question, Patrick remained quiet. At least here, there would be a healer to find the source of her strange behavior. Dragon Knight, Stephen MacKay's wife, Aileen was not only part Fae, but a healer.

"That's not really an answer," she complained.

Giving a nudge to his horse, Patrick moved across the bridge and into the bailey of Urquhart Castle. Even with snow falling, the children of the Dragon Knights scampered about in glee. Some of the boys were tossing out balls of snow while holding on to their wooden swords. Life here teemed with prosperity, and as always, an ache of longing embraced Patrick.

This is what Leòmhann requires. Not a cursed home.

Angus strode forward. "What brings ye away from the comforts—" The man paused as he regarded the lass and then returned his gaze to Patrick. "Did ye encounter troubles?"

"Not my intention when we set out for Urquhart." Patrick shifted. "We came upon the lass with a few of King John's men."

"Bloody bastard!" Angus fisted his hands on his hips. "Where? How many?"

"Near our lands. All dead."

Gwen trembled in his arms, and Patrick pondered if she was recalling the ordeal she had endured.

Stephen MacKay approached near his side. "Who is dead?"

"King John's men," confirmed Angus.

"Lugh's balls!" blurted out Stephen. "When will this end?"

Angus shrugged. "Affairs between these two kings will never cease. Furthermore, King William must be made aware of this current skirmish. I shall send a messenger to him."

"The king is nearby?" Patrick was stunned by this revelation.

"Aye. Traveling in the glen for the Midwinter feast," replied Angus. "He will spend the winter at the castle of Cormac Murray and his wife, Eve, before journeying north. Moreover, our clan shall all rest easy after our move to Aonach Castle in the spring."

The trembling which began earlier now continued in earnest with Gwen. Concerned, Patrick dropped the reins and motioned toward Owain. "The lass is in pain. Can ye remove her from my horse."

Her tremors now turned to loud snorts of laughter. "This is comical. Really, *really* hilarious." Waving a hand through the air, she continued, "I'm in an alternative universe. I grant you, it is a very interesting one. Kings, skirmishes, *Dragon Knights,* and children carrying swords? Next, you'll be telling me that the Loch Ness monster does exist."

A hushed silence descended in the bailey. Even the

children ceased their actions.

Patrick turned his gaze upward, trying to grasp a slip of patience. "Owain, *please* remove the lass before I fall off my horse."

Gwen hiccupped. "Drats! I'm sorry." She dropped his arm. "I forgot about your injury."

"Injury?" echoed Angus and Stephen.

"Arrow wound," replied Patrick, returning his attention to his hosts.

"Sweet Mother Danu." Stephen raked a hand through his hair. "I will go fetch Aileen. She can tend to the wound."

"What he requires is a doctor trained in medical procedures," announced Gwen, accepting assistance from Owain off the horse. She tucked a damp curl behind her ear and continued, "Not another person putting a blade that has been thrust into fire to seal the wound. He needs stitches and antibiotics. I hope you have a vehicle to transport him to a hospital or urgent care."

Stephen stiffened and glanced slowly at Angus. "We have a problem."

Patrick grimaced as he dismounted, pain slamming from his shoulder into his neck. "Problem?"

Angus went to reach for him but stayed his motion. "Left or right side?"

"Left shoulder," responded Patrick, noting the wariness in the elder Dragon Knight.

The man clamped a hand on his right shoulder. "Best to get ye inside and tend to the wound. We can talk further in private."

Frowning, Patrick nodded. While he followed the man, Gwen stood rooted near the horse. He paused and asked, "Are ye coming?"

Stephen stepped in front of him and dipped his head in greeting to her. "Welcome to Urquhart. I am Stephen MacKay. And ye are called?"

Blast the man. Patrick was unable to see anything. Was the lass scared?

"Do not worry, my brother will tend to the lass. What is her name?" asked Angus.

"Gwen Hywel. I ken she appears confused—" Patrick made to move toward her, but Angus grasped his arm, forcing him to step away.

"Strange clothing, speech, and appearance. Aye."

"As I was saying, I reckon she took a tumble or hit her head after her encounter with those loathsome men."

"A possibility," mused Angus, leading him inside the castle.

Angus' wife, Deirdre greeted them on the bottom stairs. "Goodness, Patrick. What brings you away from Leòmhann during this time of year, especially with snow? Mind you, it's always a pleasure seeing you—" Her eyes grew wide. "Are you hurt?"

"Aye, beloved," interjected Angus. "Go fetch Aileen and her healing supplies."

"Yes, of course." The woman smiled and hurried upstairs.

A niggling of familiarity wove into Patrick. However, the pain inside his body clouded him from trying to perceive any meaning from the woman's speech. When they finally reached a chamber, his steps slowed, and he let out a sigh as he entered.

"Bed or chair?" asked Angus, releasing his hold on his arm.

He gave the man a scornful look. "I am nae dying." Crossing the room, Patrick settled into a chair by the blazing hearth.

Angus rubbed a hand over his beard. "Anything ye can share about this Gwen Hywel? Why she was traveling alone? Where are her kin?"

Patrick leaned his head back against the chair. "Nothing." Then he bolted upright, ignoring the blinding pain accompanied by his actions. "The lass did mention having to return to Leòmhann, which is odd."

"Truly? For what purpose? Were ye expecting guests?" Angus moved across the room and reached for a jug off the table. Pouring some wine into two cups, he returned and presented one to Patrick.

Taking the cup, Patrick drank deeply. "Nae. And certainly *nae* females."

"'Tis fortunate ye came upon her when ye did." Angus took a sip of his wine as he took a seat across from Patrick. "What possessed ye to make this journey?"

Stretching out his legs, Patrick studied the man over the rim of his cup. "We required mead for the Midwinter feast."

Angus roared with laughter and smacked his hand on his thigh. "And Alex let ye leave? His second in command? What reasons did ye give your *laird*?"

Patrick grimaced. *Aye, I should have remained at Leòmhann.* "The weather has been fairly warm, and I told him the truth." He took another draw from his cup.

"And?"

"I grew restless. I blamed it on the recent clashes with King John's men. I merely sought to fetch some mead and gather any information."

The chamber door swung inward and halted any further conversation with the Dragon Knight.

Deirdre entered, followed by Aileen carrying a basket. "I've spoken with your man, Owain, and he told me how he removed the arrow barb and sealed the wound," stated Aileen. "How horrid, but you do realize I might have to reopen the wound?"

"'Tis good to see ye, too, *Lady* Aileen."

The woman narrowed her eyes. "Really, Patrick? *Aileen* will do."

Patrick smiled at her. "I leave my shoulder in your healing care."

"Good. I think it would be best if you moved to the bed. It will make it easier for me to inspect and clean the wound."

"I've brought a jug of heated water and cloths." Deirdre set a large tray on the table. She grabbed some cloths and went to Aileen's side.

After making his way to the bed, Patrick sat on the edge. Both women fussed over him as they removed his cloak. "I am honored by all this attention, ladies."

"When was the last time ye were in the company of a female, MacFhearguis? And I do not mean the one ye brought on horseback?" inquired Duncan MacKay, strolling causally into the chamber, followed by Stephen.

"My affairs are none of your concern," replied Patrick dryly.

Mirth danced within the eyes of the second eldest Dragon Knight. "So there have been *many* women recently?"

"Nae! I was merely stating that *if* there were—"

Duncan held up a hand. "Yet, that is not what ye

professed."

Aileen let out a hiss when she pulled back his torn tunic. "I believe I'll have to lance this, Patrick. It needs to be properly cleaned and stitched."

Relieved to end the current topic of conversation about bedding women with the Dragon Knight, Patrick waved his hand for her to continue. "Do what must be done, oh wise healer."

She drew back. "How much have you had to drink?"

"One cup," declared Angus.

Frowning, Aileen regarded him for several heartbeats.

Sighing, Patrick braced his hands on either side of the bed. "And nae food."

"Tsk, tsk," Deirdre admonished. "I'll go see what Delia can prepare and bring you a tray of food."

"More wine," urged Patrick.

"Bread and broth," Aileen interjected. She pointed a warning finger in front of Patrick. "No more wine until you've eaten and rested."

He shot her a twisted smile. "Mead? 'Tis why I made the journey."

Aileen gave him a horrified expression. "You risked traveling in the snow for mead?"

Duncan shoved a fist against his mouth, attempting to squelch the laughter, but failing miserably. Angus merely stared at him, his face a mask of stone, and Stephen gazed at the ceiling. Patrick was not amused. He expected at least one of the Dragon Knights to give him their support.

Patrick straightened. "When I departed Leòmhann, not a flake of snow had dusted the ground."

"We have had a mild autumn," declared Angus, folding his arms across his chest.

Aileen dismissed his remark with a wave of her hand. "Regardless, you men all know the weather in the highlands changes as often as the sun and moon rise in the sky."

The men kept silent as the woman readied her items on the side table next to the bed.

Patrick observed a *sgian dubh*, a bone needle and thread, several vials, herbs, and bandages. His trust in the healer was absolute.

Returning to his side, Aileen fingered the material of his tunic. "We need to remove this so I can wrap the bandages afterward."

Angus and Duncan approached. While Patrick lifted his arms, he gritted his teeth on the burning pain scorching his left side. Each man took care in removing the garment from his body.

Duncan rolled up the material. "Until your tunic can be mended, I can give ye one of mine."

"Thank ye," muttered Patrick, bracing his hands back onto the edge of the bed. He followed Duncan's movement out of the chamber, not keen for the next part of the plan. He knew the woman was a skilled healer, but his strength began to ebb.

"Tell me more about the woman with you," encouraged Aileen, placing her cool fingers on his shoulder.

"Her name is Gwen." His fists clenched when the blade sliced through his skin, only adding more agony. "Found...*found* her being questioned by vile men belonging to King John along the border of our lands." Patrick closed his eyes, bringing forth the images of the small lass when he came upon her. Though fear showed within her pale eyes, there was also fire. Never before had he been drawn to a female like Gwen. Perchance, it was her fighting spirit. Or skin as radiant as the first snowfall of the season. He preferred a woman with long tresses, but Gwen's honey-brown curls framed a face that bewitched him. From the moment she sat astride his horse, Patrick was eager to feast on her mouth. When he kissed her palm, she awakened his lustful beast.

Patrick shook his head to rid her image from his mind. "A strong lass," he offered softly and opened his eyes.

Angus held his gaze. "'Tis fortunate ye came upon her when ye did. If ye had not ventured out from Leòmhann, the lass would surely be dead. Or worse, on her way to King John."

Dread rose inside Patrick from the man's words. His actions to leave his home had resulted in Gwen's rescue. Concern filled him. Did she not ask if he was her savior or demon? And did he not state she was under *his* protection?

Honor, duty, and a flicker of wariness battled for control within him.

"Where is Gwen?" asked Patrick, doing his best to refrain from asking anything further.

"Being cared for by Brigid," reassured Aileen.

He lowered his head on a sigh. "Good. Duncan's wife."

For the first time since they met, Patrick longed to be Gwen's savior. And the possibility terrified him.

Chapter Ten

"Defend your honor with your dying breath, but never give your heart to another." ~MacFhearguis Motto

Stretching lazily, Gwen rolled over onto her side. After stifling a yawn, she opened her eyes. Sunlight streamed through in a golden arc from the window within her room, illuminating the lush tapestry hanging above the hearth. The fire had died down to glowing embers, snapping every so often.

Gwen bolted upright, glancing in all directions. She blew out a breath and rubbed her eyes. "I'm still embroiled in this alternate reality."

After the woman called Brigid settled her into her room, Gwen had searched the entire place for something to give her a clue to prove all of this was a ruse—merely a medieval play reenactment for visitors. She had never visited Urquhart Castle, but she bet her life this was not the same castle she had witnessed in photographs and paintings.

When the woman suggested she join them in the Great Hall for a light meal, she feigned weariness. In truth, her nerves and all that had transpired had finally taken its toll on Gwen. Sleep battled for hunger, and she succumbed to the warm room and soft bedding.

She drummed her fingers on the fur covering. "No

phone. No modern plumbing. No electricity. No heated water, unless you consider boiling water over an open flame to bathe. Now that was an experience last evening. And let's not forget, the place is barren of all present-day technology." Even the ivory shift she wore resembled nothing she had ever seen before.

Gwen shoved the covering from her body and dangled her feet over the bed. A pair of slippers took up space on the floor, and she slipped them on her feet. All traces of her clothing had disappeared, but she spied a plaid blanket draped over the chair by the hearth. Moving away from her bed, she retrieved the small blanket and wrapped the material around her shoulders. The sunlight beckoned her forward, and she wandered to the arched window.

Gently pushing back more of the wooden shutters, Gwen stood on tiptoe and studied the landscape through the barred window. Her view of the loch was spectacular. Though the morning was brisk, she welcomed the dawn's fresh air along with the chorus of birds singing. Autumn colors blended in with the starkness of white covering the landscape. A picturesque contrast.

"Serenity," she whispered. "If only I had my paints or loom to weave."

Gwen leaned against the stone. She had to remind herself that even if this seemed real, she had to find a way back to her reality. It was imperative if she wanted to keep her sanity.

Soft knocking jolted her out of her thoughts. "Come in."

When the woman entered her room with her arms full of clothing, Gwen blinked. This woman was petite and with short hair, too. She might be dressed in medieval fashion, but there was something about her that made Gwen pause. Hope blossomed. *Perhaps this is a place for travelers to experience a medieval castle. This would explain everything. But what about Patrick, his guards, and those horrible men I encountered?*

"Good morn, Gwen. My name is Fiona, wife to Alastair MacKay. You'll meet him later. He's with our children." The woman busied herself with arranging some garments at the end of the bed.

Gwen remained fixed to her spot by the window. "Where's my clothing?"

Fiona waved her hand dismissively. "Dirty and required cleaning. Besides, you can't go around wearing those garments here."

The woman's words overshadowed Gwen's joy. She fisted her hands on her hips. "Why not?"

Fiona turned to face her. "Not proper. If you prefer trews, I can see what Deirdre can have stitched for you. Although, the women and I do wear trews while training in the lists, and when the men aren't present. We choose our times wisely. Our husbands tend to become overbearing, loud, and seemingly distracted by our choice of clothing."

"They're called jeans. And I *prefer* them."

The woman angled her head to the side, a small smile flickering on the outer corners of her mouth. "I'll see what I can do. For now, I have brought you some of my gowns, chemises, undergarments, and shawls."

"Yours?"

Fiona motioned her toward her. "Yes. I hope you don't mind. Brigid said you were about my size."

Realizing her earlier rudeness, Gwen stepped away

from the light and made her way to the bed. She fingered the soft material of one of the gowns. Muted colors of greens and lavender suited the woman. "Thank you."

"You must be famished." Fiona held one of the dresses up to her. "When you're dressed, I can show you to the Great Hall to break your fast."

Gwen wanted to protest, but her stomach answered first with a loud grumbling.

"I guess I was correct in my observation?"

"I'm so confused," Gwen blurted out.

Fiona frowned. "To eat or not? Delia our cook makes a fine porridge with sliced apples."

Gwen huffed out a breath and sat on the edge of the bed. "No." She gestured outward. "Here. This place."

"Urquhart Castle?"

Chewing on the bottom of her lip, Gwen debated on what to say to the woman. "I'm almost positive Urquhart does not look like this."

Fiona pursed her lips and placed the gown back onto the bed. "What is the vision of your castle?"

"One which is in ruins."

The woman inhaled slowly and exhaled. "And one day it shall be. Yet, this is not that day. Let me help you into some clothes. After you break your fast, I will have you meet the other women."

Stunned by the woman's confession, Gwen merely nodded, allowing her to help her into the gown. Afterward, Fiona retrieved some combs from a pouch on her belt and led her to the chair by the hearth.

"I like to keep my locks short as well. Let me stoke the fire into life, and then I can tend to your hair."

Gwen fingered the material on her body. The

intricate detail of sewing was exquisite. Beautiful designs graced the billowed sleeves and hem. "This is truly a work of art," she professed.

"Brigid is the seamstress." Fiona straightened from the hearth, brushing her hands off. "Do you sew?"

"Only tapestries."

"A weaver?" Fiona's question held a note of curiosity, yet, she offered nothing more.

Giving the woman a weak smile, she responded, "Yes."

Fiona returned and squeezed her hand. "You must share more later." Picking up one of the combs, she proceeded to tame Gwen's unruly mass of curls. "Wait until you see the tapestries in the Great Hall. They were made by my husband's mother."

Gwen stared into the flames. "Will I meet her, too?"

The woman paused. "Sadly, she passed many years ago. In addition, Alastair's brothers have shared that my husband bears a striking resemblance to her, as well as his sister. But she is no longer with us."

"Is she dead, too?"

When she remained silent, Gwen glanced up at her. A touch of sadness flitted over the woman's brow, and she regretted the question.

"No. She lives." Fiona wandered to the table and placed the comb down. "She and her husband live far away from here."

Standing, Gwen brushed out the folds in her gown. "Again, thank you for your kindness."

"You shall find it in abundance here." Fiona went to the door and opened it wide. "You'll feel refreshed after food and drink."

Gwen relaxed her shoulders and gave the woman a smile. She was correct. Food and drink would help revive her spirits. However, the many questions that kept tumbling through her thoughts were going to find answers. Either she was insane, or worse. This was her new reality.

And Gwen refused to believe in the latter.

****

After finishing two bowls of the best porridge, cream, and apples she'd ever devoured, Gwen took a stroll along the Great Hall. Fiona stayed with her for a short while, and then made her apologies, explaining her new babe required feeding. Apparently, Fiona was not the only one with a new baby. The healer, Aileen, had delivered a baby in early summer as well. Unable to recall all the names of the children, Gwen gave up and concentrated on the core of the family.

As she drew near the first tapestry, Gwen marveled at the delicate, but simple stitching. What drew her attention were not the men, but the dragons that surrounded each of them. "I recognize you as the man Patrick called Angus. You have the element of fire behind you."

Strolling along to the second, she tapped a finger against her mouth. "Storms linger about you. Fiona said your name is Duncan." Pointing to the third, she smiled. "And you are Stephen. We have met."

Her brow furrowed, and Gwen took a step back to examine the fourth tapestry in a wider view. Something about the man intrigued her. He stood on the land with a commanding presence. "Have we met?"

"I believe I would have remembered the meeting," announced the low male voice behind her.

Gwen twirled around so fast, her legs twisted within the fabric of the gown. "Oh!"

Strong arms reached out to steady her. "Have ye not broken your fast or are ye feeling unwell?"

She gripped his arms, feeling utterly foolish. "Yes, I've eaten." *I'm not accustomed to wearing long gowns, but I'm not confessing that to you.* "You startled me."

The man released her and dipped his head. "My apologies. Welcome to Urquhart. I am Alastair."

"Yes, Fiona's husband."

Obviously, the man standing before her was the same in the tapestry. Yet, his appearance was one of a man who had seen many battles. A wicked scar began from his left brow and extended down his cheek. She glanced at the tapestry and back to the man. As customary on meeting someone new, Gwen would have presented her hand in greeting. However, this custom appeared foreign in this area of the highlands as evident when it came to many here in the castle, including Patrick. A stab of guilt plagued her at not asking Fiona how he was doing.

Stepping away from the man, Gwen twisted her hands together. "Do you know how Patrick is feeling this morning? Were they able to treat his wound properly?"

"Aileen is a skilled healer. She lanced, cleaned, and stitched the damage to his shoulder. He is resting, but she fears he has taken a fever."

"Then he must have antibiotics. I can't imagine why no one has suggested taking him to a nearby hospital."

"I can assure ye all is being done to see the MacFhearguis healed."

What was wrong with these people? "I don't mean to overstep, but does Aileen have a license to practice medicine?"

His face creased into a sudden smile, softening the look of the man. "She is more skilled than any, including your own."

Gwen gaped at the man. Was he mocking her? "I'd like to see him?"

"Perchance later."

Deciding it best to halt any further conversation on Patrick's condition, Gwen returned her attention to the tapestries. "These are lovely. I can tell they were made when you and your brothers were young. If I may ask, where is the one of your sister?"

Alastair's good humor vanished, replaced by a somber expression. "Aye, ye are correct. We were all much younger. There are two more, which are hanging in her chambers. If ye wish, I can have Fiona take you there to view them. She has shared that ye are a weaver."

Gwen smiled. "Yes. I have my own business in Wales. It's small, but I've recently been commissioned to weave a family tapestry for the Winter Solstice." She turned toward Alastair. "I know you don't have a phone here, but would it be possible for someone to take me to the local village? I really need to make a telephone call to them."

The man looked at her in bewilderment. "The snowfall will make it impossible to travel."

She decided to press him further for information. "Considering the terrain around here, you must have a four-wheel drive to get to places. What about food? Any other supplies for the castle? Are you self-sufficient?"

Alastair folded his arms over his chest. "We have everything we need until spring."

"*Spring*?" she squeaked, taking a step back.

He gestured Gwen toward the doors. "Why don't I take ye to the women. Brigid and Deirdre are in the kitchens."

Gwen quickly composed herself. "I know the direction. I think I'll stay here for a while longer."

After giving her a curt nod, the man exited the Great Hall.

Rubbing her arms around her body, she waited until his footsteps receded and went to the entrance. "Nothing is making any sense." For several moments, Gwen considered saddling one of the horses and fleeing.

Drawing her shawl more firmly around her shoulders, she went to the front doors and pushed them open. Icy wind and snow brushed against her cheeks. She shivered and glanced over her shoulder. If she fled, Patrick would be left in the hands of people who believed they were doing their best in healing. But what if they were wrong?

Gwen would never forgive herself if Patrick's health deteriorated. Regardless of her unexplainable circumstances, the man had saved her life. She cast her gaze on the swirling snowflakes blanketing the ground.

"Are ye thinking of leaving?" asked a female voice behind Gwen.

Jolted from her thoughts, she turned abruptly. The young girl stood near the stairs, cradling a cat in her arms. Each stared intently at Gwen. *I cannot leave Patrick.* "No." And with her decision made, she closed the doors and leaned against them.

"Who is your friend?" inquired Gwen, finally moving away from the entrance.

The girl stroked the cat's head. "Unsure. She has yet to tell me her name."

Sifting through all the names Brigid told her regarding the children, Gwen deduced who the girl might be. "Are you Nell?"

Beaming, the girl nodded. "And ye are Gwen."

"You are correct." Approaching the girl, she took in the appearance of the cat. "Do you know how she lost her leg?"

Nell lifted the animal in front of her and peered into her eyes. "Again, she refuses to share anything with me."

"Or she is frightened," suggested Gwen, running a finger over the soft fur. "She is a beauty. If she doesn't tell you her name, maybe you can call her Shadow. Her gray color reminds me of shadows at dusk."

Tucking the cat back against her body, Nell smiled "Ye speak like my mother."

"Should I take that as a compliment?"

The girl shrugged. "I do not ken the word."

Were these people disconnected from the outside world? Gwen grew weary of trying to communicate with them. "Will you do me a favor?"

"Aye. Ye are our guest."

Gwen placed an arm around the girl's shoulder. "I'd like to see how Patrick is feeling."

Nell's brow furrowed in concentration. "He sleeps."

She would not be dismayed. "Since he saved my life, I feel I owe a debt to the man. I cannot wander around this great castle. I require something to do. Do you understand, Nell?"

The girl brightened. "Follow me."

Buoyed by success, Gwen proceeded to ascend the stairs after Nell. Passing her room along the corridor, she almost laughed out loud at the irony. Patrick's room was directly across from hers. The girl placed a finger to her lips. "Our secret."

Confused, Gwen whispered, "But why do we have to keep silent?"

Glancing around the corridor, Nell acted as if she was about to impart a great confidence. "I heard my uncle and father state ye are not to go near Patrick until his fever breaks."

She cupped the girl's cheek. "Your secret is safe. Now go."

Gwen watched as Nell silently disappeared around the corridor.

Worry and anticipation clawed at Gwen. She was more determined than ever to see to Patrick's health and welfare. Reaching for the latch, she prayed she'd find the man alone. Opening the door, she slipped inside and quickly sealed herself inside the room. Firelight basked one side of the room in warmth, while a cool breeze drifted in from a partially open window. She heaved a sigh of relief, fearing they would keep the man contained in a heated enclosure and add more misery to his fever.

Scanning the room, Gwen progressed slowly across the wooden floor. Her mouth became dry the moment she gazed upon the man. Instead of being completely covered, the blanket someone had tossed over one of Patrick's legs did nothing to keep his body concealed.

She placed a hand over her racing heart as she took in the broad shoulders and dark hair dusting his chest, narrowing down the length of his abdomen. Gwen knew she should look away, but she was held mesmerized by this Adonis.

You're here to check on the man, not ogle his body.

Gwen bit her lower lip and approached near the side of the bed. Leaning forward, she examined the clean bandage. No sign of fresh blood appeared, and she heaved a sigh of relief. Tentatively, she reached out to touch his forehead. Heat poured off his skin, yet his breathing was slow and steady.

"Damn. You need medication," she mumbled.

Instantly, Patrick gripped her wrist and placed it on his chest. "What I need is a kiss from a lovely lass."

Startled, she tried to pull free. Yet, he held her firmly. "For a man with a fever you are extremely strong."

His eyes smoldered like fire. "Will ye heal me with a kiss?"

Her breathing became labored. "We've only just met. I don't kiss strangers."

Slowly, he brought her fingers to his lips, kissing each one. "I have told ye my name. What more do ye wish to ken?"

Gwen chuckled low. "I don't even know your surname."

Bringing her wrist to his mouth, he nipped along the vein, sending shards of pleasure up her arm and down her back. "MacFhearguis. *Patrick MacFhearguis.*"

Gwen swore her heart stopped beating. Lights danced in a tempest around her. "No," she whispered.

He arched a dark brow. "Aye. 'Tis my name, lass."

This time, Gwen yanked with all her might and was rewarded when he released his hold on her. All the pieces of her jumbled puzzle of insanity slipped into place with clarity. Her mind screamed at the impossibility. She refused to submit to the conclusion. He must be a different Patrick MacFhearguis. However, the further she fought the realization, the more everything became crystal clear.

Gwen required proof.

She fought to steady her nerves and clutched her hands to her chest. "What is the year?"

Patrick's brow creased. "Are ye troubled, Gwen?"

"The year!" she demanded, pounding her fist into the palm of her hand.

A flicker of uncertainty reflected in his eyes. "Twelve hundred and nine."

Hysterical laughter bubbled up inside her, and she squashed its release immediately. "How in the hell did I end up here?"

"I do not understand your meaning."

On a choked sob, Gwen ran out of the room, ignoring Patrick's plea to return.

Chapter Eleven

"Beware the canvas of your loom does not mirror the struggles in your life." ~Wisdom of the Elder Weaver

A hushed silence descended like a dark cloud on a stormy day. Adam paced furiously in front of the giant yew tree, halting to inspect the rough bark every few steps.

Meggie waited patiently for her husband to calm his temper. She cast a furtive glance at her son, Jamie. His solemn expression now a mask filled with regret and angst over the disappearance of their guest. How she longed to give both comfort—to ease father and son's agony. Patience and time was the key in this twisted occurrence of events.

Adam pounded the tree with his fist. "Give me your account *again*, Jamie."

The lad raked a hand through his dark locks, the gesture so like his father.

"I deem five times is enough, husband," interjected Meggie, coming alongside her son.

Adam closed his eyes. "Gwen has been gone for three full days. Can ye not speak with the Great Dragon again?"

"As I've previously stated, Father, she has told me this is none of her affair. 'Tis a prophecy from long ago set forth by the ancient weavers. Their connections were with the Fae."

Snapping open his eyes, Adam rubbed a hand vigorously over his face. "Nothing but a curse. And now it has taken our guest."

"I did warn her, Father," confessed Jamie, shifting uneasily.

"Can ye not share more?" Adam's tone softened as he stepped away from the tree.

"The giant yew has waited for centuries for the right person to break the curse."

Meggie studied her son. "This curse was broken when your father and I fell in love and married."

His eyes transformed into the blazing amber of his inner fire dragon. "Nae, Mother. Your destiny was aligned differently. I speak about a time when our clan settled here. The chieftain was a cruel man and did not listen to the weavers' warning."

Adam huffed out a breath in frustration and moved away from the tree. "Aye, ye are correct, Jamie. I heard my father speak often of the old chieftain and his harsh treatment of our clan."

"Ye never shared this information with me," said Meggie, reaching for her husband's hand.

Giving her a sad smile, Adam drew her to his side. "It was not on my mind when I was courting ye. And then ye...died. I buried the legend, along with my travels during the Crusades after I found ye again in the future."

He looked over his shoulder at the aging giant. "I simply forgot about the yew tree and curse."

Meggie cupped his cheek with her other hand, forcing him to meet her gaze. "We should contact the

Fae, or at the least a Fenian Warrior."

"I have reached out to *two* warriors," admitted Jamie. "Liam and Rory both have proclaimed they can do nothing. 'Tis up to the Fae weaver who looms the life threads on the spindle. Gwen dared to remove a portion of a thread magically embedded in the trunk of the yew. She is on a path no one can attempt to interfere with—unless she refuses to fulfill the prophecy."

"And this is all the knowledge these warriors imparted with ye?" asked Meggie.

Jamie pushed a rock out of his path with his boot as if mulling over more information. "I ken there is more."

"But as typical with a Fenian Warrior, they give ye only pieces of answers to your questions," confirmed Adam.

Jamie snorted, stuffing his hands into his pockets. "Aye. Ye ken them well, Father."

Reaching for his son, Adam placed a comforting arm around his shoulders. "Though there are certain times when I deem ye have more insight."

"Does Gwen have kin in Wales?" asked Jamie.

"Regrettably, she has none. At least that's what she stated to me in our conversations," responded Meggie.

Moving away from her husband and son, she regarded the yew tree one last time. "There is an ancient well near Urquhart that belongs to the Fae. I used to seek out the place when I was troubled, or to offer gifts during the solstices. If we can't get an answer from a Fenian Warrior, then I might be able to garner some information another way."

Adam and Jamie came to her side.

She glanced at Adam. "Since I know ye are not fond of driving in vehicles, I'll take Jamie with me."

Adam's mouth tightened. "They are beasties, but I shall go with ye."

"Ye hate to travel thusly," scoffed Jamie, attempting to hide his smirk and failing miserably.

Meggie started to giggle, cupping a hand over her mouth to contain her own laughter. "I can count the number of times ye have ridden in those *beasties* on one hand."

Her husband gave her a warning look. "I have another suggestion."

Meggie folded her arms over her chest, doing her best to remain serious. "Pray, do tell us."

"We can get one of those motorcycles like the Fenian Warriors have," blurted out Jamie in glee.

"No!" echoed Adam and Meggie as one.

Jamie's shoulders slumped.

Reaching for her hand, Adam pulled her away from the yew tree and to the edge of the forest. After giving a short whistle, he as well as Meggie and Jamie waited. Soon, a large horse trotted forth from the trees.

He gestured outward. "We can travel on horseback."

Jamie proceeded to walk past both of them. His voice resonated within the trees. "Come, Mother. I'll go with ye in the Jeep. If Father wishes to join us, he can follow on his horse."

"Nothing wrong with spending time with my family, enjoying the view and fresh air," argued Adam, swiftly mounting his horse.

Laughter bubbled forth from Meggie, and she was helpless to contain the mirth. No matter the century, her husband would always be a thirteenth century warrior.

****

Holding his head in his hands, Patrick attempted to halt the dizziness that plagued him. He had to go after Gwen. What was wrong with the lass? She appeared confused on the year, making him believe she had suffered a blow to the head.

He lifted his head and blinked several times, clearing his blurred vision. Gritting his teeth, he made to stand. Taking in his surroundings, he noted nothing to clothe his naked body and bit out a curse. His mouth was parched, so he slowly crossed the room to a table near the window. As he braced his hands on the rough wood, he peered inside a jug.

"Water," he muttered in regret. With a shaky hand, he poured some into a mug and drank deeply. The cool liquid eased the burning fire within his body.

From the moment the lass slipped quietly into his chamber, Patrick felt a stirring of something inside him. And when she examined his shoulder, he could not believe the beauty leaning over him. Her gown clung to her shapely curves, enticing him to trace his fingers over the fabric. She smelled of apples and flowers, and he longed to feast on her full lips.

After wiping a hand across his mouth, Patrick started for the door. Regardless of his appearance, he must find Gwen. The lass was confused. She required comfort. His steps hastened.

When he opened the door, he was met with Alastair's steely-eyed glare.

"Where do ye think ye are going?" demanded the MacKay.

Patrick straightened. "I must seek out Gwen. She is troubled."

The man took in his appearance. "And ye deem to

wander the castle *naked* as the day ye came into this world? Do ye wish to frighten all the women, including Gwen?"

Patrick gave him a scathing look. "There is nothing wrong with my body."

The Dragon Knight arched a brow. "Then think of the children."

The thought sobered Patrick. "Then fetch me a tunic and trews."

"Clearly ye are with fever. Duncan left ye clothing at the end of your bed."

Glancing over his shoulder, Patrick noted the folded items. "Not the first place I would have looked."

Alastair grumbled a curse and pushed him farther inside the chamber. Closing them both inside, he went and sat in the chair by the hearth. "Can ye share why Gwen is troubled?"

Ignoring the man, Patrick went and grabbed the garments. Sitting on the edge of the bed, he slowly drew on the trews. The man gazed at him from across the chamber, expecting some kind of answer.

"Would ye like help with the tunic?" inquired Alastair.

"Must I provide ye an answer in return for the favor?"

"Lugh's balls!" Alastair pushed up from his chair and stormed to Patrick's side. Yanking the tunic from his hands, he helped ease Patrick into the garment.

"Thank ye. Now I can go search for Gwen without offending the MacKay clan."

Both turned when the chamber door opened, and Fiona strolled into the room. "Good. You've got him dressed. I've brought some broth and bread." The woman placed the trencher on the table. "Would you like more water?"

"Wine," suggested Patrick.

"Tsk, tsk," Fiona admonished. "Aileen stated only water until the fever subsides."

Patrick frowned.

"Oh, sorry. Until the fever *lessens*. Same word."

There it was again. A strange current of familiarity with words. Patrick's pulse raced, and he stood slowly. Pushing aside the MacKay, he went to Fiona. He stared at the diminutive woman.

Cropped hair, strange speech, confusion over the year. Blast! Why did he not see it sooner?

Fiona's expression remained fixed.

He glanced over his shoulder at Alastair. In spite of his current fevered condition, everything became abundantly clear to Patrick. "Gwen is from the future?" He pointed in the direction of Fiona. "Like your wife and the other MacKay women?"

The man scratched the side of his face as if he was undecided on his response. On an exhale, he replied, "Aye. From all accounts, including Angus and Stephen's, the lass appears to be from another year."

"Is this so awful?" asked Fiona quietly.

Staggering to the window, Patrick shoved the partially open shutters aside and drew in deep gulps of brisk air in an attempt to clear his thoughts. Turning around, he leaned against the ledge. "Can ye both honestly state ye were not shocked when the truth was revealed to ye both?"

A crimson blush stained Fiona's neck and cheeks. "In the beginning, I thought him a brute." Her features softened as she slowly made her way to Alastair.

Grasping his hand, she placed it over her heart. "However, my *husband* rescued me, and I fell in love."

Alastair stroked a finger over his wife's cheek. "It took a long time to feel worthy of your love, *leannán*, and difficult to fathom why ye fell for a monster."

"You are the most handsome man I've ever known. I love both—the beast that dwells within you and the man. *Forever*."

"My *dragon* adores ye," he whispered.

Patrick turned his gaze away from the loving couple. Staring at the snow-covered hills, his mind continued to sort out the current predicament.

"Try and eat, Patrick," the woman encouraged.

He merely nodded to satisfy her demand. What he required was a strong mug of wine or even better, *uisge beatha*.

After Fiona left the chamber, Alastair approached and leaned against the stone wall. "There is always a reason why the Fae send someone through the Veil of Ages. Give it time, MacFhearguis. All will be revealed."

Frustrated with the man's words, Patrick raked a hand through his hair. "We must find a way to send her back."

"*We*? Ye were the man who came upon her. Gwen has a purpose here."

Patrick swallowed. "She's in shock right now. She demanded to know the year. I did not ken her meaning. Thought her daft."

The MacKay's eyes widened. "So ye spoke the truth about the date? This is why she is troubled?"

"Aye." Patrick shook his head in utter disbelief. "Why did I not see the signs sooner?"

"If ye had, would ye have lied?"

He snorted in disgust. "I cannot say for certain."

Alastair nudged him. "Come eat. I'll go fetch a jug of mead, and we can discuss how ye plan on aiding your lass. For now, ye can do nothing. I'll send one of the women after her."

Patrick gave him a horrified expression. "She is *not* my lass. But I would welcome a large mug of your mead and assurance she has not wandered away from the castle."

Waving a dismissive hand in the air, the MacKay countered, "Nevertheless, 'tis your problem, and *yours* alone. When I return, I expect ye to have finished what my wife has so graciously brought to ye. All the women are concerned for your health, including Gwen."

Watching the man stride out of the chamber, Patrick slumped against the cool stone. "There has to be a way to send ye home, Gwen. Aye, we shall find a way. I give ye my vow."

Chapter Twelve

"Always shield your heart with steel in the presence of a female. With one word, they can slice your heart to shreds." ~MacFhearguis Motto

When she fled Patrick's room and exited the castle, Gwen's only mission was to find an escape from this madness. She skirted past wandering animals, praying she wouldn't encounter anyone. Her steps led her to a huge garden. Quiet and soothing, except for the lone shrill of bird song, Gwen thought this was her answer to a passageway out of the castle grounds. Yet, everywhere she searched only led her to a stone wall.

Pacing furiously in the garden, Gwen was determined to get away from this delusional world. She kicked a stone out of her path, trying to fathom an escape route. Apparently, all the steep paths led to a stone portion of the castle. In an attempt to pull apart vines of ivy, she managed to scratch her hands.

"Blast and double blast. Why am I always getting in scrapes?"

Confused and wary, Gwen scooped up some snow in an effort to clean and remove the blood trickling forth on the back of her hands. "I must get away from here."

A brisk wind slapped at her face, mocking her. In reality, there was nowhere she could flee. Gwen was trapped solidly in this castle and century.

Out of the corner of her eye, she noted movement near a rosemary bush. Her previous anguish diminished as she moved cautiously toward the dog. He appeared to be part wolf and missing part of one leg.

Gwen crouched down to his level. "Are you injured, my friend?"

Giving her a wide yawn, the animal proceeded to stretch out on the ground, showing Gwen there was nothing wrong with him.

"Ah. It appears that having only three legs does not hamper you. Were you born with this condition? Or perhaps a battle over a bone with another dog? An altercation with a cart?"

Lowering her head, Gwen blew out a frustrated breath. "Patrick told me the year is twelve hundred and nine. When those horrid men tried to kidnap and take me to King John—*a king* who ruled in the thirteenth century—I assumed *they* were the demented individuals, not me. I'm having an awful time digesting this new information, even though I recall Meggie mentioning a Patrick MacFhearguis."

The dog gave a low bark, and Gwen raised her head. "Is he a good man? Do you consider him a friend?" She narrowed her eyes and studied the animal, but he lowered his head back on his outstretched legs.

Standing, Gwen lifted her arms upward. "*Where* can I find the answers?"

The leaves on the ground rustled, and she listened intently to any message—any sign. Thinking back to her last day with Jamie, images of the yew tree flooded her thoughts. The massive giant beckoned her in the sunlight. And that's where everything became fuzzy and unclear.

"Were you a passageway to another time?" She chewed on her bottom lip. "Didn't Jamie mention something to me about another path?"

Wiping her nose on the back of her sleeve, Gwen plucked a leaf from a sage bush. "I'd really like an explanation as to why I'm here in the thirteenth century, so if anyone would care to impart the information, I'm listening. Or for that matter, how can I return?"

"Are ye speaking to any ghosts who may linger here or to your companion?"

Gwen jumped at the sound of the man's voice. Turning abruptly, she stared at Patrick's concerned expression. "There are no ghosts. Only me and a dog."

"Your companion is called Cuchulainn, and there are many ghosts of the past that walk the land in the Great Glen."

She observed the animal, now in a sitting position. "He's named after the great leader of the Red Branch?"

"Aye. A proud, fierce name for this champion. He has protected many within Urquhart. Do not let him fool ye with his missing leg. He is faster than others with four."

She glanced sideways at the man. Unsure of what to say, she just remained fixed on his features. So many questions burned inside her, but he must already think her mad with her earlier question about the year. She thought it best not to bring up the subject again.

He swayed in his stance, and Gwen frowned.

Concern overrode her angst, and she moved toward Patrick. "They told me you are with fever. Should you be out in this frigid air? Especially without a coat?"

The man wiped a hand over his brow. "Frigid air?"

"Cold, frosty, chilly? Do you understand now?" *This continual lack of understanding my words only confirms my worst fears.*

A smile curved the corners of his mouth. "Aye. Good Highland air."

As she gazed into his eyes, Gwen noted the man definitely exhibited the signs of a fever. They were glassy and unfocused. She drew near and reached outward with her hand. When she touched his cheek, he flinched. "I'm merely checking your temperature."

The man radiated fiery heat, confirming her suspicions. "You smell like honey."

His smile broadened. "Ye have a cool touch, lass, and 'tis the mead. Alastair was kind enough to give me one cup."

The burr of his voice skimmed over her skin, and Gwen snatched her hand away. She took a hold of his arm. "You need to get back into bed."

Patrick chuckled softly. "Are ye going to tuck me beneath the furs?"

Heat blossomed in her cheeks, but she refused to look or answer the man.

"Will ye stay and bring me comfort?"

"You're definitely not thinking clearly, Patrick. Do you think me some hussy for the taking?" She couldn't believe she blurted those words out. Shaking her head, she said, "Forget my last statement. Obviously, when your fever abates, you'll be back to your stern self."

He brought them to an abrupt halt. "I am not always so harsh."

"Seriously? Do I have to remind you of your behavior on our way to Urquhart?"

"I did not ken ye."

"And now you do?" She laughed nervously. "You know *nothing* about me, Patrick MacFhearguis."

His features grew serious, and he brought her hand to his chest. "I can learn. Ye can start by telling me why ye ran out of the chambers."

And tell you I'm from a land eight hundred years in the future? Nope. Not going to confess that to you. I'll pretend some silly female problem.

"I think one of those awful men hit me too hard on the head," she lied.

"Ye seemed taken aback by the year."

She tried pulling him along, but the man was obviously built of steel. "Not really. You need to get out of this biting chill."

Patrick lifted his hand and smiled. "'Tis mild."

His smile disarmed her barriers. She was captivated by this giant. Returning a smile of her own, Gwen tugged gently. "I will make a deal with you. Once you have recovered, I would like you to escort me around Urquhart—from the grounds to the highest tower."

He tilted his head to the side. "Even if there is snowfall?"

"Yes."

"And ye will tell me the truth about why ye fled?"

She laughed softly. "You drive a hard bargain, MacFhearguis, but I agree to your terms."

Leaning near, he gazed into her eyes and put his hand over hers. "A bargain I shall hold ye to."

Gwen's pulse raced. The man overwhelmed her senses. She brought her hand up to his cheek, and this time, Patrick did not flinch from her touch. "I am true to my vows."

His head lowered and Gwen parted her lips, anticipating the first brush of his mouth against hers.

"For the love of Lugh and all the Gods! Why are ye outside, MacFhearguis!" bellowed Duncan.

Startled, Gwen tried to remove her arm from Patrick's grip. Lifting his head, he glared at the other man. The fierceness in his sudden demeanor shocked her. Were all men so hardened in medieval times?

Duncan halted his stride, staring at her and then snapping his gaze to Patrick.

"Do not fret like an old woman, MacKay. I was merely making sure the lass came to nae harm."

Duncan surveyed him coolly. "Now why would harm befall her in the gardens of Urquhart? Is she in danger of being eaten by Cuchulainn?"

The dog gave a low growl, wandering over to Gwen's side.

Duncan approached and ruffled the fur on the animal's head. "My pardons, dear friend. Ye would have done all in your power to protect the lass, if danger presented itself."

"He's a beautiful dog," declared Gwen.

The animal lifted his head toward her as if he understood her meaning. Soulful brown eyes stared at her.

"The great Cuchulainn was rescued by my daughter, Nell. He escorts and observes any new guest who enters the walls of Urquhart."

Brushing her fingers over the dog's head, she added, "He is also a good listener."

"Aye, indeed."

Gwen regarded the other man. "No need to worry. I'll see Patrick returns to his room—*chamber*."

Stepping aside, Duncan gestured for them to pass. "Ye are fortunate to have another tend to your healing, MacFhearguis."

Patrick ignored the man and maneuvered them out of the garden and into the corridor near the kitchens. As they continued walking through the large expanse of the castle, he remained quiet. And Gwen made no attempt at a conversation either, fearing her tongue would trip over any words she spewed forth.

When they passed Fiona on the stone stairs, she gave the woman a tight smile, realizing Patrick still retained possession of her hand.

"I brought you some more broth and bread. Try to eat all of it, Patrick," urged Fiona. "The other bowl was untouched."

Gwen glanced over her shoulder at the woman. "I'll make sure."

A flash of humor crossed Fiona's face, and she gave a curt nod.

Steadily making their way to Patrick's room, he pushed open the door and steered her inside. Making his way toward the bed, he kept a firm hold on her hand.

"Do you not think it wise to drink some of the broth Fiona brought up for you first?"

He lowered himself on the bed and peered around her. "If I eat, will ye stay?"

She swallowed, touching his forehead again. "You're burning up, Patrick. I will stay until the fever breaks." Noting his creased frown, she quickly added, "When your fever lessens or goes away."

Patrick stood slowly. Lifting her chin with his finger, he responded, "Then ye will tell me everything, lass."

Gwen grasped his hand and tugged him forward. "I told you I always keep my bargains."

"Vows," he corrected.

She laughed. "Exactly. Now sit, eat, and relax."

As soon as Patrick settled into his chair, Gwen poured him a hefty amount of water. Shoving the mug in front of him, she ordered, "And lots of liquid. It will help to banish the burning within your body."

Taking the mug, he brushed his fingers over hers. "How do ye ken how my body burns?"

He held her steady gaze, and she fought to look away from the intensity in his eyes. This flirting had to cease. The man was ill. Once he recovered, he most likely would become his harsh self. Or maybe this was his real nature? Often times, when a person is taken ill, their true personality surfaces.

Gwen straightened, placing her hands onto her lap. She decided not to fall prey to his flirting. "Each person is different, but when you're sick, the body does heat considerably."

The man studied her over the rim of his mug. After taking a few sips, he placed it back on the table. Reaching for the bread, he tore a piece off and handed it to Gwen. "I will not eat alone."

She slid him a wary glance and took the offering of food.

He tore another chunk of bread and dipped it into his soup.

Gwen nibbled on her portion and watched as the flames snapped within the hearth. Every so often, she stole a glance at Patrick, not wishing to interrupt him with any conversation. He required nourishment and rest. Regardless, her mind continued to swirl with a multitude of questions. She ached to speak with anyone about this situation. At present, she had to focus on getting the man across from her to a healing stage.

"Are ye not overly fond of the bread?"

Gwen blinked and returned her attention to the man. "Excuse me?"

Patrick pointed to the spot in front of her on the table.

Glancing down, she was horrified to find she'd shredded the bread into tiny bits. "The bread is good. I have too much on my mind." She scooped up the remnants of the bread and tossed them on the trencher.

He leaned his forearms onto the table. "We can have our conversation now, if ye wish."

Gwen stood. "No. We made a bargain for after your fever lessens. To bed, *MacFhearguis*."

A mischievous look came into his eyes. "I like how ye order me to my bed, lass."

Chuckling softly, she folded her arms over her chest. *I'm not going to continue with this flirtatious bantering.* "I'm waiting."

He approached her. "For what, pray tell."

"I'm not playing this game." She tried to hide the mirth from her features. Instead, she grabbed his hand and pulled him toward the bed.

"I do love a good game," he declared in a husky voice.

Releasing her hold, she pointed once again to the bed. When Patrick lowered his head toward her face, Gwen shoved against his chest, causing him to tumble back onto the furs. "Rest."

"Ye could have injured my arm," he protested.

She fisted her hands on her hips. "A brawn warrior like yourself? Nah. If you can endure the harsh outdoors, climbing the stairs, and attempts at stealing kisses from me, then a tumble on the furs would not do you any harm."

Patrick's expression went from humor to compelling and magnetic. He swept a glance down over her body as if he had removed her clothing. Gwen's breathing hitched, and heat blossomed in places she'd never thought to experience again.

His hand stroked the furs in invitation. "One kiss for healing?"

Her mind screamed to leave and deny Patrick his wish. Her body hastily overrode the demand.

With slow steps, Gwen approached the bed. Leaning forward, she cupped his face. "I shall give the warrior one kiss."

When the first brush of his mouth touched hers, a prickling of pleasure caressed her entire body. She only meant to give him a chaste peck on the lips, but the man placed his hand on the back of her head and deepened the kiss. As his tongue sought entry into her mouth, Gwen let out a groan and dropped her hands onto his massive thighs. She opened herself to the heady sensation. The kiss promised divine ecstasy, and Gwen surrendered to the mastery of his lips.

Never before had she been kissed so seductively. Her body burned from his touch, and she hungered for more.

As he slowly broke free, she tried to bring her breathing back to normal. She stumbled back, brushing a trembling hand over her lips.

Wariness reflected over Patrick's features.

"Forgive me."

Hurt and foolishness bartered for control within. Words failed her. Straightening her shoulders, Gwen turned and dashed out of the chamber.

Chapter Thirteen

"Never weave your thread under tears of pain."
~Wisdom of the Elder Weaver

Each day bled into the next as Patrick fought the tide of fever and pain. A fog of nightmares visited him during his slumber, and his waking moments were spent battling the burning within his body. How he yearned to have the cooling touch of the woman with eyes that shimmered like the grasses in early spring around his home.

On several occasions, he thought he heard her offering words of comfort, but nae, it was another and Patrick slipped back into the abyss of darkness.

"Wake, MacFhearguis, and drink."

The order came from far away, and Patrick struggled to fight the temptation to ignore the man's accursed talking.

"Ye cannot fall back into a slumber. 'Tis time ye rose from this bed and take sustenance."

With great effort, Patrick fought the heaviness in his limbs and attempted to open his eyes. The room blurred, and he shut his eyes again.

"Nae! Stay with me, Patrick!"

He cracked open one eye. "Ye…ye must be worried to be calling me thus," he stated in a strangled voice.

Angus lowered himself on the bed next to him. "Aye. I have nae wish to ride out to Leòmhann and tell your laird his brother died on my lands."

"And in your castle," he uttered softly, smiling.

"Drink," urged Angus, tilting a mug toward his parched lips.

After taking a few sips of water, Patrick leaned back against the pillows. "How long have I been asleep?"

"Three days."

"What?" Patrick struggled to sit and was rewarded with pain in his left shoulder. He grimaced and slumped back against the pillows.

Angus lifted the mug once again toward his mouth. "Ye should have listened to Aileen and stayed in your bed. She deems the arrow barb might have caused ye more harm. Your fever finally broke during the night."

"I have taken worse," grumbled Patrick.

Shrugging, Angus stood and placed the mug on the table. "Many have surrendered to a simple cut. Ye were fortunate we have able healers in Aileen and Gwen."

Patrick rubbed a hand over his brow. Images of their heated kiss seared into his thoughts. Why did he take advantage of Gwen? Alluring, aye. But did he not promise to protect her? Even in his fevered condition, he ached to bring her onto the furs and ravish her with more kisses. He lifted his head. "The lass tended to me?"

"Day and night."

Patrick swallowed. "Has she spoken with anyone?"

"About?"

"Where she's from? Anything?"

Shifting his stance, Angus narrowed his eyes. "The

lass has kept to herself. She took her meals in her chamber or in the kitchens. The women have tried to speak with her, but she flees the moment they talk to her about her kin or where she is from. 'Tis a secret she has nae desire to share with anyone, save one. *Ye*."

Patrick glared at the man. "Alastair told ye what happened? How she was troubled when she asked the year? Can he not have kept silent?"

"We harbor nae secrets within these walls," confessed Angus. His tone held a bitter edge of scorn. "As Alastair has told ye, there is a reason *Gwen* has traveled here through time. Ye must determine the meaning and assist her in her task."

"Aye. To find a way to return her to her time," added Patrick, pinching the bridge of his nose to ward off weariness. He deemed three days was long enough in bed. Come the morn, he'd force himself to heal. Enough of foolish thoughts and stolen kisses. Gwen had to return to her own time.

"I heard mentioned Gwen stated she wanted to return to Leòmhann. Ye might begin your questions with why she wished to seek out your home."

Patrick lifted his head and studied the man. "Aye, *aye*." Then he bolted upright, disregarding the shards of pain. "By the hounds! Leòmhann—Adam and Meggie?"

Angus narrowed his eyes and rubbed a hand over his chin in thought. "Perchance." He pointed a finger at him. "A word of caution. Ye must tread carefully with Gwen. We cannot alter the future in any way."

Clenching his fists into the furs, Patrick's eyes blazed with determination. "I understand the risks, so ye must trust me. If the Fae have sent her back to us, she might be a messenger. There could be a problem with my brother."

A glint of humor flashed in Angus' eyes. "If that is what ye believe?"

Confused, Patrick countered, "What other possible conclusion could there be?"

A roar of laughter burst forth from the Dragon Knight. He strode toward the door. As he made to exit, Angus paused and glanced over his shoulder. "I judge there might be another reason."

"Care to share, Dragon Knight?" mocked Patrick.

"'Tis for ye to discern, my friend."

Angus' footsteps receded, along with his laughter down the corridor.

Frustration settled like snakes within Patrick's gut. He leaned back against the pillows and glanced upward. "Time to gather a plan, MacFhearguis."

He uttered a soft curse and closed his eyes.

****

Soft feminine laughter brought Patrick out of his deep slumber. Slowly opening his eyes, he gazed at the beauty on the furs by the fire. The blaze danced off her honeyed curls—her relaxed profile held mirth. She had this beguiling habit of biting her lower lip, and Patrick recalled how they tasted.

Instantly, his cock betrayed him and hardened. In an effort to tame the lustful urges, he listened to her whispering to Cuchulainn. She was sharing a story about her journey on horseback. He barely recognized some of the words—her use of the language foreign to him. She bent near and continued to speak in hushed tones. No doubt the animal had befallen under her charm.

Grateful for the trews he was wearing, Patrick rose up on the bed and rubbed a hand over his eyes. Pushing aside the covering, he brought his feet to the cold surface of the floor. No dizziness plagued him for the past several days after he had finally broken the fever. In truth, his strength was returning immensely.

Aileen refused his requests to take his meals in the Great Hall, so he used the time to rest and devise a plan for sending Gwen back to her time. Yet, he required honesty from the lass. Patrick took in a deep breath and released it slowly. The time for confessions was overdue.

Her ever-faithful guard lifted his head and gave a low bark, alerting his mistress they were being observed.

Turning around, Gwen's eyes widened. "Thank the angels, you're sitting upright."

He doubted angels had anything to do with his recovery. Patrick braced his hands on the side of the bed and made to stand. *I have been doing so for many days.*

Gwen hastened to his side. "Let me help you."

"Nae." His tone more gruff than he intended.

Hurt reflected back at him within those jeweled eyes. She turned away and started for the door.

Regret haunted him. "If I take a fall, I could bring harm to ye. Will ye stay, lass?"

Halting her stride, she turned and slowly wandered back to his side. She offered her arm. "Then take a hold of me. I am stronger than you might think."

Patrick smiled slowly. "I have seen the mighty Gwen Hywel be brave when faced with King John's men."

Her eyes lit up. "Want to know a secret?"

By the Gods, he yearned to learn all of her secrets. "Aye."

"You have no idea how frightened I was of those men and the entire situation."

Briefly, he considered confessing his worry at seeing her with those vile men. "Despite your fear, ye were brave."

She lowered her gaze. "I did scream once or twice, but more out of anger. I had never in my life been struck by another person."

Reaching out, Patrick lifted her chin with his finger. He noted the dark smudges under her eyes. Angus did tell him that she had stayed day and night in his chamber, and he pondered if she found any rest for herself.

"And ye never shall again." Though he spouted his vow to Gwen, he worried upon her return to her own time. Was it a violent period? He dropped his hand. "I judge the path to the table shall be a steady one."

She eyed him skeptically. "You are a stubborn man. But I'm happy your fever broke. I'll go prepare something for you to eat. You have missed today's morning meal."

"Can ye not stay for a while? Did ye not state that when I broke my fever ye would tell me what troubles ye? I had thought ye would have visited sooner." Patrick took a hold of her hand and placed it in the crook of his arm. He steered her toward the table, noting the wariness riding her features.

"I think it better if Aileen came to check you and the bandages."

Patrick halted their stride. "Why are ye here?"

She frowned in thought. "The other women were busy, and Aileen thought it best if someone checked on you. When I arrived, Cuchulainn was resting by the fire and I sat with him for a while." She cleared her throat as though she was considering her words carefully. "We all were worried about you, Patrick. I simply tended to you during your fevered condition."

"'Tis not what I meant, though I am grateful for your healing touch and concern. What I should have said is why are ye here in this *century*?"

Gwen tried to pull free from his grasp. "Disregard my earlier words from days ago. I was overwhelmed by what had happened when you and your men came upon me." She tapped her head. "Daft at the time."

Shaking his head slowly, Patrick led her to a chair and gestured for Gwen to sit. He would not be dismissed so easily. "Nae, lass. Ye are not from here—this time." Pulling out another chair, he placed it beside her.

She fidgeted with an empty trencher and moved several mugs around on the table. "Again, I told—"

"Ye were shocked at finding out the year, aye?"

"Don't you need to put on your tunic? It's a bit drafty in here."

"'Tis warm," he argued.

"Goodness!" Gwen reached out and touched his forehead. "Are you coming down with a fever again? I should definitely fetch Aileen."

Patrick leaned forward, blocking her path to flee. "Nae fever. Merely the heat from the fire near this table. My strength is returning." He straightened. "Though if ye find my body offends ye…"

She bit her lower lip while two bright rosy spots

stained her cheeks. "Absolutely rubbish. Nothing wrong with your…um…body," she mumbled.

A smile twitched at the corners of his mouth. "Good. Now ye can proceed with telling me the truth."

"Truth?"

"The year ye came from?"

"You wouldn't believe me." Her voice was resigned.

Patrick rubbed a hand over his beard, making a mental note to shave it later. "Gwen, I have seen evil rip apart my world, so repugnant ye would believe anything. Trust me when I say that what ye are about to profess will not shock me."

"Depends on what you consider fact versus fiction."

By the hounds, Patrick never had encountered a more obstinate female. Though he lacked the knowledge of some of her words, he suspected their meaning. As a hardened warrior, he had no more patience with bantering further with the lass.

Exhaling softly, she reached for the mug and sniffed. "Too bad this isn't wine."

His irritation lessened. "Would the drink help ye? I ken where Angus keeps his good wine."

She shook her lovely head. "No. Water will suffice." After pouring a hefty amount into a mug, she drank deeply. Refilling the mug, she handed it to Patrick.

Taking the offering, he took a sip and leaned back in his chair.

Gwen clasped her hands together and stared into the flames. "The year I came from is two thousand nineteen. I was staying at Leòmhann Castle as guests of

Adam and Meggie MacFhearguis. I was commissioned to do a tapestry of the family. The castle was newly restored after being in a state of ruins. I had only been there a couple days. My memory is hazy, and fragments are missing. To be more exact, a jumbled mess. I see a giant tree, golden light. A total mess of images."

Patrick's heart pounded fiercely against his chest, and he gripped the mug tightly. His mind attempted to process Gwen's words. *Ye have seen my brother—his wife? Our castle, our home was in ruins?*

"My last coherent image is of Jamie leading me on horseback up a hill away from the castle," she added in a rush. "Everything else is mixed up within my mind."

"Jamie?" asked Patrick in a hoarse voice.

Gwen returned her gaze to him. "Yes. He is Adam—"

"And Margaret's son." Placing the mug on the table, Patrick stood and walked to the arched window.

"How do you know?" Her question barely a whisper.

He laughed bitterly. "Adam MacFhearguis is my *brother*."

Gwen abruptly stood. "This is madness!"

"Why? Can ye account for why ye are here in my time? Nae. 'Tis not madness, but *Fae magic*." He glanced over his shoulder at her.

"But...*but* they are in the future." A frown marred her features, and she came to his side. "How can he be your brother? None of this makes any sense. You want me to believe in magic by what, the faeries?"

Rubbing a hand down the back of his neck, Patrick tried to ease the tension. He could not fault the lass in her logic. An idea took hold and he reached for Gwen's hand. "We do not call them faeries. The *Fae* are different—powerful. Allow me to show ye something."

Gwen glanced down at their joined hands. "Your fingers are warm."

"And yours are verra cold."

"Nerves," she confessed. "Or I'm in shock."

He laughed. "Then that makes two of us, for I find your story *shocking* as well."

Slowly, she lifted her head up, searching his face. "But you do believe me?"

Wariness reflected back at him within those eyes. "Aye, lass."

She let out a long exhale. "Thank you. I believe for the first time my skewed realty is real, but still inconceivable."

Patrick kissed the tips of her fingers before releasing them. "Help me with my tunic, and I shall show ye proof of my brother and his family."

Smiling broadly, Gwen dashed over to his bed and retrieved his tunic. After carefully putting the garment on, he led her out of his chambers. He kept silent as they ascended a narrow circular set of stairs. Making quick strides, Patrick found the door he was searching. Saying a prayer it was not locked, he lifted the latch and pushed it open.

Darkness greeted them, along with the ghosts of the past. "Stay here," he uttered quietly.

Crossing the room, he removed the latch from the shutters. Pushing them back, sunlight streamed into the cold chamber.

Gwen stepped inside and closed the door behind them. "Why the secrecy?" Hesitantly, she moved to his side.

"Painful memories reside here." He gripped her shoulders and turned her toward the hearth. "Look above on the stone wall."

He felt her tremble beneath his hands.

"It's them," she uttered in a shocked tone. "Meggie, Adam, and oh my! Jamie is younger in this tapestry."

An ache settled within Patrick. "Brigid tried to capture her brief memory of Jamie—my nephew—when he visited briefly. She procured the help of local weavers."

"Why is it hidden away? Furthermore, why do they have a MacFhearguis tapestry in the home of the MacKays?"

Blowing out a frustrated breath, he drew Gwen to his side. "In the beginning, when the tapestry was finished, the MacKays placed it with the others in the Great Hall. Ye see, Margaret—*Meggie* MacKay is their sister. She married my brother, Adam. As time passed, their leaving brought anguish that would not leave the hearts of the MacKays. One day, Angus ordered the tapestry removed and placed inside Meggie's former chamber here."

"I'm utterly confused, Patrick. Why are they in *my* future?"

"'Tis a verra long story, Gwen. One filled with good and bad magic, battles, death, lost love, and finally redemption."

Gwen smiled fully, bringing radiance to the dreary chamber and his soul. "I don't believe I'm going anywhere nor have plans for the rest of the day. Therefore, I'm all yours."

In that quiet moment, Patrick realized what he

needed was someone other than a MacKay or MacFhearguis to listen to his account—from battles fought, brothers lost, and unhappiness which filled not only his home, but his soul.

Though he did not believe in the new religion, Patrick pondered whether the beguiling lass was an angel sent to him.

A gift he did not deserve.

Chapter Fourteen

"An oath can never be broken, not even by death."
~MacFhearguis Motto

Hours passed as Gwen listened in rapt attention as Patrick spoke of an incredible tale detailing the Dragon Knights—men with elemental powers who were part Fae, and the MacFhearguis clan. Both clans were sworn enemies for many decades. When a great battle was fought against an evil druid, both families united in their quest against the evil. Since then, the Dragon Knights and MacFhearguis clan became allies and good friends.

As she sat curled up on a pillow under the arched window in his chamber, she wept tears several times, and Patrick gently brushed them away with the pads of his thumbs. The story was one for the ages—an account of epic proportions for both these clans. In the end, not only did her heart ache for everyone in this century, but for Adam and Meggie in the future. Ripped apart by evil—yet brought back together with love and magic. Regardless, they could never return to the past.

After Patrick finished, he let out a sigh and stared outward at the loch.

"So, Nessie is actually a Great Dragon brought here by the Fae and now resides in Loch Ness. Astonishing."

"How does my brother fare?" he asked softly.

She leaned against the stone and regarded the profile of this rugged Highlander. "Apparently, Adam is a happy man. In truth, all of them are one big happy family. The children—"

Patrick leveled his shocked gaze at her. "Children?"

"Jamie and Alexander. In addition, she is pregnant with a third child. I don't know their ages, but if I had to guess, I'd say the boys are thirteen and ten."

Patrick chuckled softly. "Nae.'Tis the Fae blood in the lads that makes them appear older than their years. Good to hear another son has entered their lives and more to follow."

Gwen held up her hand. "Please, do not tell me any more about the Fae. My head needs time to digest all this information."

A glint of humor creased his face. "No matter the years, I still find it hard to fathom, and I grew up around the Dragon Knights, magic, evil, *and* the Fae."

She tucked her legs under her. "What about Christianity?"

"The new religion has found a place here in the Great Glen, but not among the MacFhearguis and MacKay clans. We accept the change sweeping across the land but continue to follow the old beliefs. Nevertheless, Adam did embrace the new religion."

"Yes, of course, since you stated he went on the Crusades. I can't imagine what he witnessed."

"Carnage, violence, evil. All in the name of the one God. He returned home more broken than when he left."

Wishing to offer him comfort, Gwen reached out

and touched his arm. "It's in the past. He is now extremely happy. Anyone can see how happy they are just by looking at them. They seem to have this silent connection with each other. I witnessed it on several occasions during my short time with them. True love shines in both of them."

Cupping her chin, he leaned forward. "Your words have brought a small amount of peace into my soul. I thank ye."

His touch and nearness heated the small alcove under the window. Never before had Gwen been so powerfully drawn to a man. Once, she thought love had entered her life. Yet, it was foolhardy nonsense, especially when the man left her after their one night of sex. She swore an oath no man would claim her heart or body again. Love existed only in faerytales.

Regardless, here she sat in a medieval castle with a Highlander, and her heart blossomed each time she gazed into his eyes. She tried many times to squash the feelings—blaming it on her circumstance, or the fact he had rescued her. But this emotion was too powerful to ignore.

"Then that makes me happy," she admitted.

"Tell me of your life, lass."

She rubbed her nose. "Goodness, my life is boring. My parents died when I was young, and I was shifted from one family after the next. It was a revolving door—at least that's what I came to believe. Simply passing through a family for a brief period of time. Often times, I didn't feel welcomed." Huffing out a breath, she added, "But that part of my life is over. I now own a company that restores and creates tapestries. I live in a small loft above my store."

"'Tis good to hear the old ways have not been forgotten in regards to weaving." Patrick gestured toward the tapestry. "They are a window into the past." For a moment, he remained silent before blurting out, "Are ye *married*?"

Gwen laughed. "You'd be surprised how much the world has changed." Glancing away, she said, "I've never been married. I don't believe it's in my future, either. I'm destined for a life alone."

"Can ye be content without a husband? Nae bairns to fill your life?"

Fidgeting with the folds in her gown, she returned her gaze to Patrick, unable to answer him. "Do you have a wife?"

"Nae."

"Perhaps we're fated not to have anyone." Yet the words she spouted rang untrue within her heart. Gwen had always hungered for love and a family. Even when she visited Adam and Meggie, she coveted what they had. And being around the MacKay family wasn't any better. A constant reminder of a life she longed for but might not ever have. Maybe God thought she didn't deserve this kind of life. Obviously, she didn't truly have one growing up, so why did she believe she could have a relationship and all it entailed as an adult?

"I am a hardened warrior, *leannán*. 'Tis not possible for me to have what my brother possesses."

"Why? Have you done something so awful that you're unable to be worthy of love?" Uneasiness twisted like gnarled vines within her stomach.

"Doomed from the actions of my ancestor." His mouth thinned in obvious disgust. "I cannot undo the past."

Determined to find out more, she pressed him for more. "You're wrong. Whatever this ancestor did, it has *nothing* to do with you."

He pounded his chest. "His cursed blood travels in my veins. I can find no comfort in a wife and bairns. Death would cloak them and all who enter Leòmhann."

"Superstitions," she argued, wanting to wrap her arms around the man and banish his fears.

Sadness creased his brow. "They are as real as the air ye breathe."

Resigned, Gwen looked away. How could she make sense to him? He had his Gods and Goddesses, the Fae, and beliefs she couldn't fathom to decipher. Maybe there was something she was supposed to do for him, and this is why the angels or Fae sent her back to his time.

She drew in a breath and released it slowly. "Life is measured by what we can do for others. If we take happiness along the way, can we not return it to another? I choose to believe in the goodness of a person's soul and not the bad deeds of a family member being passed down from one generation to the next. Genetics is one thing, but deeds? No."

"Ye have brought me happiness by sitting and talking to me. I ken the meaning of some of your words, but ye must understand how I view life."

She tilted her head to the side, marveling at his features. He was a study of dark and light, hard lines and soft edges. A man conflicted with the past, present, and future.

"I do understand," she uttered quietly.

Silence enveloped them. There was nothing more she could say to convince him.

Lifting his hand, he tugged on one of her curls, and his eyes smoldered with desire. "I have stolen kisses from ye, Gwen, and asked for one in a fevered condition. Now I shall ask if ye will permit me to take one, given freely by a woman to a man?

Her pulse raced. She knew the answer without having to dwell on the ramifications of her emotions. "Actually, all my kisses to you have been given freely. So yes, you may kiss me."

His lips slowly descended to meet hers. She trembled at the sweet tenderness of the kiss. When she placed her hands on his chest, he let out a growl and deepened the kiss. Gwen opened fully to him, their tongues battling an exotic dance. His fingers skimmed along the top of her breasts, finally cupping one in his hand. As he continued to fondle and tease her, desire rolled through her and to places she'd never experienced. She yearned to strip her gown and have him touch her in the most intimate of places on her body.

His kiss was like a drug, and she craved more than just the one.

Gwen broke free, breathing heavily. Scooting closer, she traced a finger along the base of his neck. Leaning forward, she kissed the vein, eliciting another powerful growl from the man.

"I fear one kiss is not enough," he admitted, his brogue thick along with the heavy erection jutting against the material of his trews.

"Agreed," she murmured, unsure of only one thought. Consequences be damned. If she traveled all these centuries back in time, why couldn't she be brave enough to give free rein to her emotions?

Patrick stood. Reaching for her hand, he brought her to standing and grabbed her around the waist. His hands burned through the fabric of her gown, and she desired Patrick more than the air she breathed. He smothered her mouth with demanding skill, thrusting his tongue deep inside. Gwen surrendered to him, and the tide of passion swept her up in its current.

He slowly backed her across the chamber until they came to his bed. Without breaking the kiss, he brought her back onto the furs. His kisses were divine ecstasy, heating her body to an exquisite fervor which could not be cooled.

When he bunched up her gown, Gwen halted his progress. "No. Your shoulder."

He arched a dark brow seductively. "I feel no pain, *leannán*. I merely wish to give ye pleasure. To feel your softness. Will ye allow me to touch ye here?"

Desire kept her tongue silent, and she simply nodded her approval for him to continue.

While his hand caressed her thigh, he nuzzled kisses along her neck. Her body trembled—going from half ice to half flame. His intimate touch left her breathing heavily, and when his finger swept across her sensitive core, Gwen arched in pure pleasure.

"I burn for ye," he whispered against her ear.

Words failed her as the man kept stroking the flame of desire within her body. Desperation clawed at her to crest in a feeling she'd never felt, and she moaned, clutching the furs. "Need more," she whimpered.

"What do you want, *leannán*?"

The timbre of his voice rippled across her skin. His question more of a demand. He thrust a finger deep inside her, but it wasn't enough for Gwen. She craved all of the man, not sweet kisses and touches. Opening her eyes, she cupped his face. "All of you."

"Are my kisses not enough?" He removed his hand and cupped her breast.

She swallowed, pushing the bravery of her actions forward. "No. I yearn for more."

Patrick leaned back, and doubts surfaced within Gwen. Had she been too brazen for this medieval man?

"Ye are willing to give me your body? Here? Now? When I cannot promise ye tomorrow?"

"We only have this moment in time," she added, unsure of any future or which century she belonged to.

"Aye."

Courage and fortitude rooted inside Gwen for the first time in her life.

Gwen tugged at the lacings in front of her gown. While keeping her focus on Patrick, she slowly undid them. When the last lacing slipped free, she slipped the gown off her shoulders. "I have never been surer of anything in my life."

His eyes darkened with desire, raw and magnetic. "Ye are more beautiful than I imagined."

When he tugged at his tunic, she helped to ease it off of his body.

Patrick bent his head and cupped both breasts in his hands. As he swiped his tongue over her taut nipples, she let out a groan. Yet, when he lavished both breasts with his mouth, Gwen shook as an unrelenting yearning built between her thighs.

When Patrick broke free, she let out a protest. Until she understood his meaning. With deft skill, he eased out of his trews and kicked the material aside. She swallowed, unable to look away from his massive erection.

"Do ye find me pleasing, *leannán*?"

She snapped her gaze to meet his. Heat pooled in places she craved for his touch. "Definitely."

He crossed the chamber and in one move, bolted the door. "I have nae wish for us to be disturbed."

She swallowed, watching as he stalked back to her.

"Remove all of your clothing," he demanded. "For I fear, in my haste, I will rip the material from your body."

Gwen's hands trembled as she complied with his order. Completely naked in front of the man, she watched in a lust-filled haze as he approached once again.

Predatory, seductive, and all male.

She scooted back onto the furs and held out her arms to him. He complied with her unspoken wish. His mouth covered hers hungrily, igniting a firestorm when his skin touched hers. He teased and tormented Gwen with his words and touch. When Patrick nudged her thighs apart with his knee, she felt the heat of his arousal near her entrance. Taking her mouth in a more savage kiss, he thrust his erection deep inside her. Her cry resonated inside him, and she fought the desire to wrap her arms around his shoulders.

"Ye are a vision and tempt me beyond words." His breath blew hot against her cheek.

She fisted her hands in his hair, urging him onward. When he bit the soft spot below her ear, she arched madly. Dizziness swamped her vision as a wave of immeasurable pleasure tore through her body.

He captured her scream with his mouth, stealing

her breath and returning it mingled with his own.

Patrick gazed down at the beauty beneath him. With each thrust into her feminine core, a part of his heart splintered. Powerful, hungry, desire rippled through him. He spiraled into an abyss of passion he'd never experienced. Unable to hold back any further, Patrick emptied everything he had into Gwen. His growl of release echoed off the chamber walls.

Moments slipped by, each trying to regain their breathing.

Carefully, Patrick rolled onto his back bringing Gwen to his chest. He caressed his hand over her back, treasuring the feel of her against his body. As his breathing returned to normal, Patrick closed his eyes. Bliss and contentment filled his spirit.

Until he heard her whispered question.

"What now, Patrick? Why was I sent here?"

Words he wanted to express lodged like a lump of bread in his throat. And his vow to see her safely to her own time left him unsettled. He opened his eyes to find her staring at him. They shimmered in the fading light within the chamber. Patrick was enchanted with the lass. "I have nae answers."

"Nor I," she acknowledged with a sigh.

He kissed her softly. "Then let us share the rest of the night together. Perchance when morning arrives, we shall have our answers."

Gwen's smile broadened in approval.

Gliding his hand down her backside, he cupped her bottom and squeezed gently. "Ye shall not find sleep tonight, *leannán*. Only pleasure."

Chapter Fifteen

"Bed many women, and remember, love none."
~MacFhearguis Motto

On a yawn, Patrick opened his eyes and searched for Gwen. Blinking several times, he turned over. Crumpled sheets greeted him, but no sign of his *leannán*. With a groan, he rolled back against the pillows and tossed an arm over his eyes. He was foolish thinking she'd be here in the morn. Images of the MacKays crashing down his door and demanding answers came unbidden to his mind. And he had none to give them, if they had appeared.

Furthermore, her scent lingered everywhere—from the furs to his body—Gwen surrounded him, including a part of his heart. The tiny, fierce woman had invaded his blackened and hardened shield in their brief time together.

"I was meant to be your protector, nothing more." He blew out an exasperated breath. Tossing the furs aside, he then sat on the side of the bed. Rubbing a hand vigorously over his face, Patrick deemed he needed to clean up and leave this chamber. He had been prone far too long, though he didn't mind some of the time spent with a lass who had beguiling eyes.

Her question from last evening tumbled back within his thoughts. He still had nae answers. "What shall I do with ye, Gwen, lass?"

Leaving the comfort of the bed, he searched for his discarded trews and tunic. Quickly dressing, Patrick made hasty strides out of his chamber. As he approached Angus' solar, he gave a soft knock on the wood. Silence answered him, and he followed the corridor and descended the stairs.

Duncan stood leaning against the entrance to the Great Hall, speaking quietly to Stephen. Both men halted their conversation as Patrick approached them.

"Good to see ye have left your chamber," acknowledged Stephen, clamping a hand on his good shoulder.

"I remained there upon your wife's instructions," responded Patrick dryly, sorely tempted to utter a harsh retort about being treated like a weak lad.

The man snorted and dropped his hand. "My wife is the healer."

"How are Owain and Andrew?" Patrick shifted his stance, half expecting his men to appear forth from the Great Hall.

"Currently out in the lists, though they have asked morn, noon, and evening after ye."

"They are good men. I thank ye for seeing to their comfort."

"'Tis good to see ye have recovered and left the bed chamber," greeted Alastair, coming alongside him and handing him a mug. He leaned near and uttered in a low tone, "I've poured ye some mead, but keep silent or the women will lash out at me."

Patrick took the mug, grateful for something other than water or wine. Taking a sip, he savored the honeyed liquid. Alastair made the best mead in all the

Great Glen.

"Is there something ye wish to confess?" asked Angus, emerging from behind Patrick.

Sputtering on the mead, Patrick glared at the Dragon Knights gathered around him. He would not disclose anything to these men. He had the impression they all knew his secret—that he'd bedded Gwen, but they would never hear his confession. *Ever.* "I require a shave for my beard and a clean tunic."

Angus clasped his hands behind his back. His eyes studied him like a hawk. "I meant your conversation with the lass."

Smiling despite his inner turmoil, Patrick took another sip of the mead. "We have talked. I am trying to devise a plan to send her back to Leòmhann in the present."

"Sweet Mother Danu," hissed out Stephen, grabbing Patrick's arm. "We kent she was from the future but thought she had tumbled through the Veil of Ages to your home in this century."

Patrick wiped his mouth with the back of his hand. "Shall we take this discussion into the hall?"

"Aye," agreed Angus, gesturing for him to proceed into the hall.

Once they were all gathered around the long table near the blazing hearth, Alastair poured some more mead into Patrick's mug and shoved a trencher of bread and cheese in front of him. "If any of the women see ye drinking and not eating—"

Patrick held up his hand to stay the man's words. "They'll have your heads."

All the Dragon Knights nodded in unison.

"Continue," urged Alastair.

Leaning back in his chair, Patrick raked a hand through his hair and set his mug on the table. "Gwen was consulted to stitch a tapestry for Adam and Meggie's family."

"By the hounds," muttered Duncan. "She has seen our wee sister."

Patrick's smile was sad as he added, "And they have another son, Alexander." Tearing off a chunk of bread and cheese, Patrick stuffed the food into his mouth.

Alastair lifted his mug in salute. "Good news to a new bairn."

"Aye," echoed the other Dragon Knights quietly.

Patrick nodded his sentiments as well. "Meggie is carrying another bairn, too."

Quiet settled around the men. Patrick deemed the Dragon Knights all fought their own despair over the loss of their sister. He prayed this bit of news would lift their sullen spirits and bring some peace to their souls. As the years bled into the next, each man refused to discuss Adam or Meggie in an open discussion.

"Do ye fear for your brother and our sister?" Stephen asked quietly. "Do ye reckon this is why the Fae sent Gwen to ye? Did she share what she was doing before coming to us?"

Scratching his beard in thought, Patrick instead looked at the eldest Dragon Knight. Angus regarded him with steely calm. No trace of emotion reflected in the man's eyes. If Angus deemed Adam and Meggie were in trouble, the Dragon Knight would do all in his power to travel through time and come to their aid. He reached for his mug and drank deeply. After finishing the mead, he shrugged. "She only recalls traveling with

Jamie on horseback among the hills around our home. Her memory is unclear."

Angus leaned back in his chair and folded his arms across his chest. "Ye must aid her in recovering her memories. The message is for ye."

Glaring at the man, Patrick responded, "What makes ye so sure?"

His reaction appeared to amuse the Dragon Knight. "Ye found the lass."

"A chance encounter," Patrick argued, reaching for the jug of mead.

The table erupted into snorts and laughter. Patrick glanced around at the men. Clearly, they found his opinion unbelievable.

As Patrick poured a hefty amount of mead into his mug, Alastair nudged him. "I suggest ye eat more. Fiona stopped by the entrance."

This time it was Patrick who chuckled. "Your back is to the door, so how can ye ken who was standing there?" He drank deeply, ignoring the stares from the other men.

"I can *sense* my wife from some distance," replied Alastair in a harsh voice.

"Bloody Fae senses," snapped Patrick and placed the mug down. Not wishing to continue with the present conversation, he asked, "Has the snowfall decreased?"

Angus rose from his chair. "Nae. Ye and your men are most welcome to spend our last Midwinter at Urquhart with us." He motioned to Duncan and Stephen. "I need to strengthen one of the stable walls and require your aid."

Patrick's eyes widened. "Are we into December?"

"Aye!" declared Alastair. "The women have

already been preparing, though the feasting is several weeks away."

Duncan let out a groan and stood. "The daily lists will be too numerous to count." Following Angus out the hall, he continued to utter words of protest.

"Ah. But think of all the tempting foods, Brother," suggested Stephen, running after him.

"When do ye depart from here?" asked Patrick between bits of cheese and bread.

"Early spring. We had planned on leaving this year but judged it best to forestall until the birth of the bairns this summer." Alastair added in a somber tone, "We shall leave the ghosts of the past within the stones for another."

Patrick studied the man. "Aye. A shame Meggie did not impart why she made this request for ye to leave your home."

Alastair scratched his beard. "She had nae wish to impart too much knowledge about the future. We had to trust in her sage advice."

"Aonach Castle will be a grand home." Patrick gestured outward. "From what I've seen, it will be bigger than here."

The Dragon Knight's mouth twitched with amusement. "To provide for an ever-growing family."

Eating in quiet reflection, Patrick settled his thoughts. His own brother would be spending Midwinter alone. An ache of regret for leaving Leòmhann sliced through him. A rash decision sped him onward to the home of the Dragon Knights, not even considering the repercussions.

But what if Angus was correct? Was Gwen sent here—to him? For what purpose?

Patrick stole a glance at the man sitting next to him. "What are your thoughts on Gwen?"

"Are ye sure ye want my thoughts?"

"Did I not ask ye?" Although he was hesitant of hearing the Dragon Knight's conclusions, Patrick wanted another's opinion.

Leaning his forearms on the table, Alastair nodded slowly. "The lass is destined to be here, either as a messenger *or* for another purpose."

"Which is what?" demanded Patrick.

Before Alastair could respond, Gwen entered the hall, carrying a tray with cups. Her steps slowed as their gazes locked, and Patrick found he was unable to look away. Each time she smiled or laughed, the darkness retreated within his soul. Her lavender gown hugged her curves to perfection, and images of their lovemaking slipped through his mind.

Gwen was as radiant as the heather that graced the hills in autumn, her face as white as snow on a winter day, her laughter as gentle as a spring breeze, and her scent as intoxicating as the summer wildflowers.

Rising from his chair, Patrick slowly made his way to her. He lifted the tray from her hands and placed it on a nearby table. "Ye left early?"

Gwen darted a glance around the room. "Of course."

"Without a kiss of farewell?"

Two patches of roses bloomed on her cheeks. "I did."

Footsteps sounded behind him, alerting him to Alastair's presence. The man dipped his head in passing to Gwen. He paused at the entrance. Glancing over his shoulder, he said, "Ye already have your answer,

MacFhearguis."

Patrick gave the man a curt nod, unsure of how to respond.

"Are you the one now troubled?" asked Gwen, touching his arm.

Confused is the word I would have chosen. "Nae. Merely having to reflect on being here at Midwinter and not with my brother."

Startled, Gwen took a step back. "We cannot go back to Leòmhann?"

"Too treacherous with the heavy snow. The main pass will be unachievable."

A frown creased her lovely face. "I understand. So, how long must we stay?"

"Does this news bring ye distress?" Uncertainty wove its way inside of Patrick.

"Yes. I mean *no*. Blast! I don't know what I'm saying anymore." Gwen shoved past him and walked toward the hearth.

Making quick strides to her, Patrick placed a gentle hand on her shoulder and turned her toward him. "Was last night a mistake, Gwen? Did I bring shame to ye?"

Her eyes widened. "Now I'm confused. Why would you bring me shame?" She looked around the hall before returning her focus to him, adding, "I have never experienced such passion."

Patrick fought the temptation to sweep her into his arms. Instead, he trailed a finger over her soft cheek. "Truly?"

Her lips parted. "Yes. There is no shame in what you did to me. I enjoyed it all."

Leaning near her ear, he whispered, "Then will ye come to my chamber tonight?"

Gwen placed a hand on his chest. "How long are we staying at Urquhart?"

Placing his hand over hers, he replied, "Until the snow melts."

She arched a brow at him and took a step back, leaving him chilled. "Which means late winter or early spring?"

"Correct," he acknowledged and dropped her hand. Her questions and tone unsettled Patrick. Desire sparked between them, so why was the lass hesitant?

"Patrick?"

He blinked, returning his attention to her. "Aye, *leannán*?"

"I'm trying hard to figure all this out, including this new element—*you*." Darting around him, Gwen began to pace. "I'm a list maker. Everything is organized in my life. Now it appears as if I've stumbled through time and into your world. This makes everything complicated—*difficult*. My emotions are scattered."

Fear clutched at his heart. "Again, I ask if last night was a mistake?"

Fisting her hands on her hips, she narrowed her eyes. "Obviously, we are having a problem with communication. No, it wasn't a mistake! And I don't deny wanting you again, Patrick." She slashed the air with her hand. "But I don't know what's going to happen in a few months. So we continue to see each other every night, until I find a way back to my time?" Stepping closer, she cupped his face and her scent filled him. "I'm afraid I'll have feelings for you and then be snatched back to my own time. It's not fair for either of us."

Icy tendrils swept down his back, jolting him back

to reality. Her words slashed at him. Did he not profess only the one night? And here he was trying to lure her into his bed for several months. *Ye are a fool, MacFhearguis. Ye made a grave error in bedding the lass.*

Patrick faltered in the silence around them. The sheer truth was Gwen would return to her own time, most likely upon their return to Leòmhann. His feelings were lustful and had to end.

"Say something," she pleaded.

Fisting his hands at his side, he gave her a curt nod. "Ye are correct. It would be foolish to bed ye anymore."

"Right. Um. Yes. *Foolish* is the correct word, though a bit harsh."

Without giving him time to make amends, she turned and hastily darted from the hall.

Raking a hand through his hair, Patrick let out a soft curse. Never in his life had a woman left him dazed, confused, and utterly forlorn over the loss.

Chapter Sixteen

"Often times, your loom can mirror your current life and become a tangled mess. Stitch with caution as ye move from left to right." ~Wisdom of the Elder Weaver

"Two bloody weeks," protested Gwen, smacking the wooden table in the kitchens. The man was insufferable, refusing to even speak with her when he entered a room. She was irked by his cool, aloof manner each time they met.

In truth, she should be grateful Patrick chose to ignore her. "I thought I knew him better," she uttered with dismay. "Men are all the same, regardless of the century." She muttered the last words and let out a frustrated breath.

The cook, Delia clucked her tongue in disapproval of Gwen's rant as she continued to stir the stew over the open hearth.

Plucking a rosemary branch from the table, Gwen twirled the fragrant herb between her fingers. After their heated conversation in the hall, she had kept mostly to herself and the animals. Her only exception was during the evening meals. The MacKay clan was a lively, happy family, and Gwen became fascinated with their interaction. Laughter flowed as heavily as the mead and wine. She found herself looking forward to the evening and the banter of conversation between them.

And Patrick was as elusive as a feather on the wind. Slipping in and out of the hall—from speaking quietly to one of the men, to snatching some food off a trencher and leaving. Her heart plummeted each time he left.

Did she truly expect Patrick to be jovial toward her? Entertain her with more stories of his family and those of the MacKays? Whisper words of enticement to her in secret? Or steal kisses in the darkened corridors when no one was looking?

Her body demanded his attention, but her mind slammed the door on any invitations.

The duel of emotions left her frustrated and fatigued. By the time she climbed into her bed each night, Gwen succumbed to pure mental exhaustion. Yet, even in sleep she found no solace. Instead, she dreamed of passionate kisses and touches that drove her into a frenzied state of desire.

"It's only lust, nothing more. And since I spurned any future advances, I can't blame him." However, the words left a hollow ache of denial. She cared more for Patrick than she cared to admit.

She gathered a few more rosemary branches. Slowly securing the sprigs with twine, she tossed them near the others. Her thoughts returned to their dull and disquieting mockery over Patrick's silence.

"Wonderful. You're almost done," exclaimed Brigid, dangling another basket of herbs around her arm.

Startled from her depressing thoughts of the man, Gwen moved aside. "More rosemary?"

Brigid leaned against the table. "No. Pine branches. Would you like to work on something else? Fiona and Aileen are making kissing boughs for the castle."

"Kissing boughs?"

Without waiting for Gwen to respond, the woman linked her arm with hers. "Yes." Moving them steadily out of the kitchens, she added, "It is a custom here during Midwinter. We place them *everywhere*." Brigid sighed dreamily. "Some of the best kisses from Duncan were under those boughs."

As the woman prattled on, Gwen listened with intent. For weeks, she wanted to ask these women where they hailed from. Each spoke with a distinct accent. Without wanting to appear rude, she asked, "What part of Scotland are you from? Is it the north? Or do you hail from one of the outer islands?"

Brigid snorted and clapped a hand over her mouth. "Sorry," she mumbled.

While they continued along the corridor, Gwen waited for her to answer the question. As silence reigned between them, her patience appeared to snap. Was it a horrible secret? Did the woman flee from a miserable life and family? She grew weary from all the secrets.

Patrick only mentioned the MacKay men. Not one word did he spew about these odd women.

Gwen shook her head. "Forget I even asked the question. I was curious." She quickly chastised herself for the rudeness in her voice.

"On the contrary," stated Brigid. After leading her up a second set of stairs, the woman halted before a door to their right. "From my conversation with Patrick, he has not confessed to you his knowledge of where we came from."

"I presumed you lived in various parts of the country." Curiosity spurred Gwen on. "Do you have powers like your husband?"

Brigid gave her a wry smile. "You could say ours is the power of knowledge, which we must keep to ourselves." Opening the door, she gestured for Gwen to step inside.

Entering the large room, Gwen took in all the beautiful tapestries. Though these were much smaller than the ones in the Great Hall, the craftsmanship was detailed and stunning. Scenic landscapes with animals graced many along the walls.

"We love this room," announced Fiona, who sat in a large chair near the window. Sunlight illuminated the woman while she worked on the kissing boughs strewn about on a large table.

Gwen smiled, feeling a connection to this other petite woman. While she wandered along the table, she brushed her hand over the various sizes of twigs, ribbons, and fruit spread out in an orderly fashion.

Brigid dumped the basket of pine branches near Fiona. "Deirdre and Aileen will be joining us shortly. They are tending to the children."

"Two were born this year?" inquired Gwen. She took a seat at the far end of the table.

Fiona leaned back in her chair. "Yes. I had another son, Niall. We named him after my oldest brother. And Aileen gave birth to another son, Simon." She sighed heavily and brushed a lock of hair out of her eyes. "We all kept praying for girls."

Brigid laughed. "I don't think that will happen again."

Confused by the woman's comment, Gwen asked, "Why not? Are daughters not favored?"

Brigid pulled out a chair beside her and sat down. "Absolutely. But they are rare among the MacKays. When Aileen gave birth to twins—one a girl—it was considered a blessing and a change in the clan."

"Yet you have a daughter," countered Gwen.

Brigid reached for a lavender ribbon. "She was taken in by the MacKay clan, along with my son, Finn, after the death of their parents. My husband came upon them after a fierce storm. Nevertheless, in my heart I love both as if I had given birth to them."

Fiona reached for a pine branch. "Regardless of longing for a girl, I do love my sons. They're strong, stubborn, and with tempers to rival their father's."

"Indeed," agreed Deirdre entering the chamber, followed by Aileen.

Sighing, Brigid twirled the ribbon between her fingers. "I so miss Finn."

"Where is he?" asked Gwen.

Tears misted the woman's eyes. "He went to go live with Fiona's brother and wife on an island off the coast of Scotland. He wanted to further his training as a warrior with them."

"He could have made the journey this year," complained Fiona.

Brigid wiped away a tear that had slipped down her cheek. "He is on his own path. When he is ready, he'll return home."

Unsure of asking any more questions, Gwen simply nodded. Love truly abounded here at Urquhart.

As soon as the other women were gathered around the table, Brigid turned toward her. "Regrettably, this is not the main reason I've brought you here."

A flicker of unease swept through Gwen. They were regarding her like some specimen. Had Patrick confessed her secret? Did they want to know what the future might hold for them?

"We've waited for the right moment to discuss your situation. Actually, we expected you to share or come forward with your concerns."

Gwen's shoulders tensed. *They knew she was from the future. He told them.*

Brigid placed the ribbon on the table. "Since you're going to be with us for a lot longer than you or Patrick had planned, I judge it wise to share our backgrounds."

"How can that help me return to Leòmhann?" blurted out Gwen, unable to hold back the words.

"Because you're not the *first* to tumble back in time," uttered Fiona softly. "It is a secret we've all had to keep."

The light of the woman's words slammed into Gwen, and she rested her gaze at those gathered around her. "Each of you has traveled back in time?" She barely recognized the sound of her voice.

Fiona stood and came to her side. Dropping down beside her, she grasped her hands. "For me, I was born in this century, but sent to the future as a small lass. I won't bother giving you the details, except to say, I was sent away from my family for my safety. Most of my life, I sensed a longing of something missing. Until I slipped through the Veil of Ages and landed in medieval Ireland—the country of *my* birth."

"*Veil of Ages?*" she asked trapped in a hazy confusion.

"Somehow, you slipped through a portal of time,

which our husbands refer to as the Veil of Ages."

Gwen lifted her gaze to Deirdre. "And you?"

The woman placed her hands on the table. "I was a famous mystery writer, born and raised in San Francisco, California. Yet, the real chapter of my life didn't truly begin until I met Angus. I slipped through to the past while on vacation in Scotland."

Aileen coughed into her hand. "So poetic, Deirdre."

"Of course, *half-Fae* lady."

Gwen looked at Aileen. "What? You're a Fae?"

Smiling, the woman nodded. "On my father's side. He was a great warrior in his world. This is why I have a special gift for healing. Regrettably, I found all this out at the end of his life. I was born in Scotland but raised in Boston. I slipped back in time through a passageway at the ruins of Arbroath Abbey."

"I'm sorry for your loss," professed Gwen.

Fiona stood. Placing a hand on Brigid's shoulder, she said, "And this lady was the first."

"Strange, it seems so long ago," declared Brigid. "One moment, I'm arguing with a Fae Warrior and running through the trees near Aonach Castle, and the next, I'd landed in thirteenth century Scotland."

Deirdre pointed a finger at Brigid. "You bet the Fae messed with all our lives to bring us to our men."

"Thank the Gods and Goddesses!" exclaimed Aileen. "There was a purpose to why we were sent, along with the message which was given to each of our husbands."

"Message?" echoed Gwen, enthralled by their confessions.

"It was so long ago, and I've forgotten the words.

We were chosen to help them on their paths," answered Aileen, easing back in her chair. "The Fae are powerful. You were sent for a purpose, Gwen. Whether you choose to accept the path is entirely up to you. Remember, there's *always* a choice."

Confusion over her emotions for Patrick and this sudden revelation from these women had Gwen's stomach flipping like butterflies. "I miss a good cup of tea," she confessed quietly.

Aileen chuckled. "Coffee for me. Oh how I miss the strong brew." She closed her eyes. "If I pretend hard enough, I can smell the aroma."

Fiona giggled. "I miss running *hot* water."

"Tired of hauling the pail or finding someone to fetch some water for you?" teased Deirdre.

"Definitely! Or when I want to clean up the children. What about you?"

Deirdre sighed. "Coffee *and* my laptop. There are times when I want to research something fast."

Brigid raised her hand. "I miss bathrooms and toilet paper."

"Yes!" They all echoed in unison.

Gwen burst out laughing. Weeks of pent up emotions tumbled free, and soon she was doubled over in laughter. After several moments, she recovered and wiped a hand over her brow. "Goodness. I needed to release some of this tension."

Brigid stood and walked to the window. She leaned forward as if searching for someone. Finally, a smile creased her features. "No matter the hardships and what we've all endured, I wouldn't trade anything for the love I hold for Duncan." The woman glanced over her shoulder at her. "I'd go through the suffering and heartache all over again. This path is your own, Gwen, especially during the Winter Solstice—a season of hope *and* light."

Gwen fidgeted with the pine branches on the table. Love emanated from all of these women. They had men who worshipped them. Patrick only wanted her in his bed—nothing more. He was correct in that aspect. It was foolish to think of anything else.

And her heart ached at the realization.

If you can hear my prayer, Fae, please find a way to send me home. My heart is in serious danger of being hurt.

****

Alastair sipped his mead while observing Patrick hidden in the shadows of the Great Hall. The man remained rooted to the ground and his position, refusing to approach any of the tables. Apparently, he was waiting for a certain lass to enter.

Duncan nudged him. "What is holding your interest?"

"The MacFhearguis."

"Why has he not joined us?" Duncan reached for a trencher of bread, ripped off a piece, and handed the rest to Angus.

Alastair smirked and took another draw of his mead.

"Is there something ye care to share with us?" asked Angus.

Stephen strode forward and settled across from them. "Where is Patrick?"

"The man has become attached to the stone wall," replied Alastair, setting his mug on the table and staring at his brothers.

"Whatever for?" demanded Stephen, sweeping his gaze outward.

Before Alastair had a chance to respond to his brother, the women entered. Musical laughter floated inside the hall. Even with the appearance of Gwen, the MacFhearguis remained a frozen statue.

Stephen leaned forward. "What is wrong with him?

Alastair gave his brother a passing glance. "The man is enchanted with a certain lass. He's stalking her like she's his prey."

Stephen choked on the bread he had shoved into his mouth. Recovering quickly, he asked, "How do ye ken?"

Scratching the side of his face, Alastair replied, "Can ye not see he has shaved and cut his hair? From the moment the lass entered the hall, his body went rigid. Trust me, soon he will begin pacing."

"If he intends on acting in this manner, we are in for a long winter," complained Stephen.

"By the hounds," hissed Alastair. "Ye are correct." Reaching for a jug of mead, he poured some into two mugs.

Arching a brow, Stephen surveyed his brother. "What are ye doing?"

"Getting him to take a stance and remove himself from the shadows."

Stephen blew out a curse. "Plying the man with drink will not help him."

"If ye have a better solution, do share."

His brother smirked and waved him away.

Making steady strides across the hall, Alastair winked at his wife in passing.

Patrick swiftly removed his attention from his

current obsession and looked at Alastair. Handing the man a mug of mead, Alastair chided, "Do ye plan on staying in the shadows this evening?"

"Would ye be bothered?" Patrick took the offered drink and leaned back against the wall.

Alastair narrowed his eyes in thought. "Hmm. Considering ye are a guest at Urquhart, I have nae desire to see ye miserable."

The man appeared affronted. "I am not."

"Liar."

Patrick let out a hiss. "Tread carefully, Dragon Knight."

Alastair fought the smile forming on his face. "Then why do ye not sit with your men? Or with us?"

"I grew bored with the conversation."

"Tsk, tsk." Alastair glimpsed over his shoulder. He understood he was poking a bear, but the MacFhearguis required prodding to move forward. Returning his focus to the man, he inquired, "So it has nothing to do with Gwen?"

Patrick glared daggers at him. "'Tis none of your affair."

"Contrary to what ye may think, this sullen behavior does not go unnoticed. And all that happens under the roof of Urquhart concerns everyone."

"If ye must ken, I am duty-bound to return Gwen to Leòmhann, and unless we have a warm winter, I fear the months ahead." Patrick swirled the mead in his mug. "Do ye think ye can speak with Duncan and suggest having him thwart any storms coming into the glen?"

Alastair choked on his mead. "Lugh's balls, nae! My brother would have to spend the entire winter on the north wall deflecting the storms."

"I am merely asking for a week, nothing more."

Sighing, Alastair rubbed a hand down the back of his neck. "Can ye share why ye would fear spending the winter here?"

After draining his cup, Patrick shoved it back at Alastair. "I thank ye for the mead and conversation."

"Patrick, the Fae are far more powerful than ye may think."

"And your meaning?"

Alastair clamped a hand on the man's shoulder. "Halting the storms across the glen will not stop the path ye and Gwen must tread."

Chapter Seventeen

"With sword, shield, and loyalty, always remain steadfast toward family." ~MacFhearguis Motto

Raking a hand through his hair, Patrick blew out a frustrated breath. Alastair's words still echoed within him after he had ventured out of the hall last evening. He remained conflicted with his feelings for Gwen—a constant battle between his body and mind. "What message do ye bring from the future, *leannán*?"

He bent and retrieved a rock. Tossing it with all of his strength, he watched the stone skip three times across the loch. Memories of his brothers challenging each other in this exact way unfolded within his thoughts.

"Move aside, Adam. Ye are too skinny and have nae muscle in your arm," scolded Alex. "Let me show ye how it is done."

"Why must ye always be first," protested Adam, glaring at his brother.

"Because I am the oldest and stronger."

Patrick snorted in disapproval. "'Tis skill, not strength."

"Hold your tongue," warned Alex.

"Why? Do ye think to frighten me with the same words ye spew at our baby brother?"

Adam stomped the ground. "I am not a baby! I am

seven years!"

Patrick placed a fist over his heart, trying desperately to keep from laughing. "Forgive the reference, youngest brother."

Picking up a stone, Adam narrowed his eyes. "I have been practicing daily."

Alex shoved past him and made for the edge of the loch. "Ye must wait your turn."

"Bastard," whispered Adam.

Patrick held up a warning finger and stepped near him. "Ye are fortunate Alex did not hear ye curse him."

The lad lifted his chin in defiance. "I do not fear him. He will not become laird."

"If anything happens to Michael, Alex will be the next laird."

Adam spat on the ground. "Evil always lives a long time."

Regrettably, their older brother, Michael was a cruel man and becoming laird at a young age did not endear him to their people or family. To hear Adam spout what they all held within their hearts left a hollow ache inside of Patrick.

"Are ye watching?" shouted Alex from the shore.

Patrick nudged the lad. "Let us see how our older brother fares and then ye can go next."

Adam's eyes widened in surprise. "Ye will let me go second?"

"Are ye deaf?"

Puffing out his chest, Adam shook his head. Grinning from ear to ear, he darted near Alex and waited.

As Alex tossed the stone outward, Patrick held his breath. The stone rippled across the water only four times before splashing into the water. "Not your best."

Alex shrugged and turned around. "Better than ye."

"Patrick said I can go next," announced Adam.

Alex shot a hard glare at Patrick but remained silent.

Folding his arms over his chest, Patrick watched his little brother whisper over the stone he held in his palm. Taking a step back, he shot the stone across the water.

And on that glorious spring day, Adam became the champion of skipping stones—his stone bouncing off the water five times.

Patrick sighed heavily. "The youngest became the wisest on that day. Ye taught us that skill is often times more valuable than strength. How I miss ye, Adam."

"His path was the most challenging *and* rewarding," stated a familiar voice behind him. "Destined to become a Dragon Knight and bring about a new order."

Turning abruptly, Patrick smiled broadly. "Cathal!" He almost shouted his response in surprise at seeing a good friend.

"'Tis good to see ye, too," chuckled the man.

After embracing the druid, Patrick stood back. "The MacKays did not mention ye were traveling to Urquhart."

The druid glanced outward with a somber expression. "I would not have missed their last Midwinter feast at a home which has seen generations of their kin. I found a calling to return and journeyed swiftly to make it before the feast day."

"Then the snows were light on your travels?"

"Aye. Until recently." Cathal stroked a hand through his gray beard. "And 'tis good ye are here as well. Did Alex make the journey with ye?"

Patrick drew in a breath and released it into the frosty air. "Nae. When I left my home, it was a vow to return within a week. It has now been a month. Circumstances beyond my control have kept me here."

"The snowfall," affirmed Cathal. "And?"

Giving the druid a skeptical glance, Patrick shrugged. "I rescued a lass along the journey and became injured. It was fortunate we were near Urquhart."

"Hmm. Ye look mended and nothing appears to be broken. But a lass?"

"She is from the future."

Thumping his staff onto the ground, Cathal burst out in laugher.

Patrick waited for the druid to compose himself. He required wise counsel from the elder, not humor.

After wiping a hand over his brow, the druid moved along the edge of the water. "So another one has slipped through the Veil of Ages. Do ye ken the reason she was sent here?"

Keeping pace with the druid, Patrick replied, "Nae. Do ye?"

Cathal halted. "Why would I ken the purpose?"

"Ye can speak to the Goddess and the Fae. Surely, they will offer their wisdom to a great druid. Or were ye shown a vision of her arrival from the Fae?"

"Do not flatter me with your words. Ye can offer your questions just as easily to the Fae," he spoke softly. He pointed his staff to a limb on a mighty oak tree. "Who can say why this lone leaf has not fallen?

Sometimes the answers to our questions are easy, and others take time to reflect on them." Turning around, he aimed his staff at Patrick's chest. "What ye seek is inside here. Ye will not find your answers in your mind, unless you understand them in your heart."

"I am conflicted," confessed Patrick, bending and picking up another stone along the water's edge. "As ye ken, our family does not do well with keeping women happy. Leòmhann has long suffered—"

"Bah!" interrupted Cathal. "'Tis time ye and Alex stop thinking of the past." He gripped Patrick's arm. "If ye continue to dwell on the misfortunes of others, ye will never break free."

The druid's strength and words stunned Patrick. He regarded the man for several heartbeats. "I have made a vow to return the lass to her home. What can I do?"

"Stop allowing fear to guide ye," suggested Cathal.

"Patrick?"

Cathal instantly removed his grip from Patrick, and both turned at the sound of a certain female's voice.

Gwen ducked under a tree limb, heavy with snow, and Patrick became a young lad beguiled with her beauty and grace.

"I'm sorry for intruding. I heard voices and thought I recognized one of them." There was wariness in her tone as she swept her gaze to both of them.

"We were simply discussing foolish thoughts," mentioned Cathal.

Patrick clenched his jaw. *Nae foolish! Conflicted!*

She frowned. "My apologies for interrupting."

The druid dipped his head in greeting. "I am called Cathal, druid to the MacKays. I bid ye welcome." Cathal cast him a speculative glance before returning his attention to Gwen.

Patrick remained rooted to the ground, unable to move or speak. He grew tired of battles, ghosts from the past, and curses. Just once, he longed for a beacon of hope to fill his life. A chance to cast off the misdeeds his ancestors had left behind. And he missed being with Gwen—his heart and soul weary from keeping his distance from her.

The lass beamed. "Why thank you. My name is Gwen."

The druid touched Gwen's basket. "Are ye foraging for mushrooms?"

"Yes. I found some nestled against an oak under the snow."

"Ye have some beauties in those ye have gathered."

Patrick cleared his throat. "Are ye all alone out here?"

Her smile vanished, and Gwen darted him a glance. "Yes. Except for the occasional rabbit or deer. Is that a problem?"

By the hounds, she despises me. I bedded her and then spurned her. "Nae. I presumed ye to have..." He coughed. "What I meant to say is, would ye like some company?"

Chuckling softly, Cathal started for the path leading to Urquhart. "Enjoy your walk. I shall enjoy conversing with ye later, Gwen."

She looked at Patrick in surprise. "I would welcome the company."

Determined to keep her good spirits from faltering, Patrick bounced the stone in the palm of his hand. "Would ye care to wager how many times I can skip this stone over the water?"

The corners of her mouth twitched in humor as she moved forward. "Are you aware I do not have coin on me?"

Keeping stride with her, he countered, "I have nae interest in coin."

She stooped down near a tree and brushed the snow away from the base of the trunk. "I'm afraid to ask what would interest you."

Leaning against the tree, Patrick studied her features. Heavy lashes shadowed her rosy cheeks, and he longed to trace his finger over her smooth skin. "One kiss, *leannán*."

She lifted her head slowly, and he noted the hesitancy in those jeweled eyes. Patrick held his breath, fearing her reply.

"Why?" Her question barely a whisper on the wind.

Conflicted by so many emotions, Patrick tried to find the simplest answer. "Because I have thought of nothing else."

Again, he waited.

Rising slowly, Gwen removed the stone from his hand and brought it near her lips. She met his gaze boldly. "For one kiss, you must skip the stone *five* times."

His pride concealed his inner turmoil. Never in Patrick's life had he been able to master the skill of skipping stones. The most he'd ever accomplished was three times. "Done."

When she dropped the stone back into his hand, her fingers brushed inside his palm, and he trembled. Patrick fought the temptation to take her full lips in a fiery possession as he closed his fist around the stone.

Stepping aside, he strode with intent to the water's edge. Determination wove a tight thread in his quest to complete the task. He cast his sight out to the expanse of water. *If ye can hear my thoughts, Fae, grant me this one request to skip a simple stone five times across the loch.*

Quieting his mind and body, Patrick lifted the stone. A shaft of sunlight broke through the gray day—light shimmered off the water in a mirror of jewels. Taking a step back, Patrick cast the stone outward and held his breath.

Hope soared within him as the stone skipped once, twice, three, four—and splashed into the water.

His shoulders sagged, and he was heartsick at the loss. Gwen approached quietly by his side. "Pity. It was a great throw."

"Aye," he acknowledged softly. "One of my best. My brother, Adam was a champion at this game. I should have studied him more."

"Interesting," she mused.

Straightening, Patrick started forward. "I can help ye pick more mushrooms. Are they for the Midwinter feast?"

"Yes. Apparently, they're for an onion and cabbage dish. Sounds delicious. I'm amazed at how all the women have managed here in this time-period."

"I had heard it was a struggle in the beginning for them." He glimpsed sideways at her. "How do ye find being here? I cannot fathom what ye must miss."

She shrugged. "There's simplicity here. I'd almost call it serenity. I've learned a lot this past month. Whereas, in my town you can go crazy trying to keep up with everything." Gwen waved a hand outward. "And don't get me started on city life. Traffic congestion, speedy drivers, people always on their cell—" She giggled. "Sorry. Too confusing for you."

Patrick smiled, trying to perceive everything the lass was saying. Each time she spoke, her face would light up. There was a musical lilt to her voice that soothed him. He found her enchanting, regardless of the words spewing forth from her.

Noting a group of mushrooms, he moved away from Gwen.

"Since you have lost, what about *my* end of the bargain? I believe I can claim something of value."

Patrick froze in his steps. Glancing over his shoulder, he stared at her in disbelief. "Ye wish to claim a reward?" Hope soared within his heart as if the sun's rays stoked the emotion.

Her tongue darted along her lower lip. "Absolutely."

He turned slowly around. "Name your reward." Tension coiled within his muscles.

She approached him in an unhurried fashion. "You might have requested one kiss as your reward, but I'll take *four*—the same number of times you skipped the stone over the water."

His heart hammered against his chest. His mind refused to understand the magnitude of her words. "*Four?*" he uttered in a hoarse voice.

"Four," she affirmed, stepping closer. "Do not keep me waiting."

In one swift move, Patrick crushed her to his chest. Her soft curves were warm against his body. "Start counting, *leannán*."

She never had a chance to respond as he hungrily covered her mouth with his lips.

Chapter Eighteen

"When ye have stitched the last thread on your loom, whisper a prayer for long life and good health."
~Wisdom of the Elder Weaver

Boisterous laughter filled the bailey—from the oldest adult to the smallest lad and lassie. Each person tried in vain to capture the ducks who had escaped from their pen. Between the loud squawking, laughter, occasional curse word, followed by a prayer, not one person was able to capture any of the elusive ducks.

Content to be a bystander, Gwen had witnessed the chaos near the garden and took shelter under the arched entryway. The snow had turned to a light rain, causing more antics to ensue when one of the men slipped and collided into another. The children collapsed onto the ground in fits of hysterical laughter.

Gwen drew her cloak more firmly around her body and adjusted her hood, observing one man in particular. Patrick appeared to be intent on becoming the winner of this fracas and did not succumb to the humor. As the time slipped by, the water on his beard turned to icicles. She couldn't decide if she liked him with or without facial hair. The man was a complex individual of layers. Each day, she thought she'd uncovered everything. And then the next, he'd surprise her with something new. Today she found out how skilled he was with a blade.

The man moved with fluidity and strength against the powerful Dragon Knights. It was quite a scene in the lists this morning. Regardless of the injury to his shoulder over a month ago, Patrick's healing, strength, and stamina amazed Gwen. One she applauded gleefully when Stephen MacKay took a blow to the chin by Patrick.

To her surprise, Patrick saluted her and blew her a kiss in front of the others in the lists.

Ever since their wager out by the loch several days ago, the man became more at ease around her. Talk of the future was squashed—mostly by her. Gwen didn't want to dwell on hopes, faery wishes, or relationships. In truth, her heart was smitten with the man, and the possibility he felt the same would be too much to hope for. What chance did they have together?

I am a modern woman and you're a medieval man. This is only temporary.

An ache squeezed within her chest at the thought of leaving him.

When she had fallen in love was difficult to determine. Yet, the emotion had woven its spell within her heart and no matter the circumstances of their situation—Gwen could no longer deny her feelings. While she loved Patrick, she had to reflect on the reasoning of why she had been sent back in time. Fragments of her memory were still missing. If only she could remember. There must have been something she did right before she blacked out. Even with the help of Aileen, she was unable to bring back her lost memories.

"Does the lady wish to make another wager?"

The resonance of Patrick's voice jolted Gwen back

to the present.

The man shook his head, water and ice flying in all directions while he moved toward her.

She shivered, but not from the chill. The man oozed a masculine charm each time he came near her.

Pointing to a duck waddling off in the direction of the garden, she replied, "I'm afraid the offending fowl will win and you will be the loser."

His eyes crinkled with mischief. "Ye fear the challenge?"

"Never," she blurted out, unsure of what he meant and quickly added, "Have you not already taken your kisses?" *And my body, too.*

Patrick crooked a finger for her to come forward.

Leaving the shelter of her protection, Gwen complied. Standing in front of him, she lifted her head. His seductive gaze bore into her, holding her captive. Her fingers dug into the fabric of her cloak to keep from reaching out and brushing a lock of wet hair out of his eyes.

"I accept your challenge," he professed.

Gwen arched a brow in disbelief. "You've spent over an hour attempting to capture one of the fleeing ducks. Why boast about taking victory now?"

He winked at her. "To give the children some fun. I cannot proclaim their fathers did the same. They understood they risked a tongue lashing from their cook if they did not gather them back into their pen."

Stunned, Gwen gestured outward. "For what purpose would you deceive the children?"

He clutched her hand in both of his—the warmth seeping into her skin. "I love to hear the sound of children laughing."

Another layer of Patrick MacFhearguis has been revealed. "As do I," she confessed softly.

Squeals and shouts broke the spell around them.

Gwen leaned to the right to witness victory. "Unless you have extraordinary skills, I believe Duncan is the winner of capturing the ducks."

Patrick drew her close. "But not the one in the garden. Furthermore, if I retrieve him, ye will dance with me at the Midwinter feast." Releasing her, he dashed into the garden.

Smiling, Gwen moved slowly to the entrance and leaned against the wooden structure. "I still say Sir Duck will become victorious in his stealthy escape."

Within moments, the man came strolling out of the garden with the duck tucked under his arm. As he neared her, he dipped a bow. "Ye shall save *all* your dances for me."

Shocked, she asked, "How in the blazes did you manage to get him?"

His mouth twitched in amusement. "Bread crumbs."

Her gaze darted to the pouch secured at his waist. "You cheated."

"Contrary to what ye have witnessed, I never cheat. Merely balanced the odds in my favor."

Gwen bit the inside of her cheek to keep from smiling. "Then dances you shall have, but nothing more."

Patrick gave her a look of censure. "Nae more of your sweet kisses?"

She flicked a feather off his drenched tunic. "All will be determined after I see how you dance."

His eyes darkened with desire. "Then I will enjoy

tempting ye. As another challenge, if ye enjoy dancing with me, I shall permit ye to kiss me. But ye must ask, first."

"Tsk, tsk. I thought we moved beyond *asking*."

"Thank goodness, Patrick!" exclaimed Brigid. "You've found the last one."

The man gave her a wink and turned to face the woman. "I will take him to his pen and see that it is latched properly."

Gwen watched as Patrick ambled away while whispering soothing words to the duck in his arms.

After viewing the earlier scuffle of trying to capture the elusive fowls, her heart grew heavy that a couple of the ducks would be part of the feast.

"A penny for your thoughts." Brigid nudged her in the arm.

She swallowed, returning her attention to the woman. "Feeling sorry for the ducks. Their end is coming soon."

Brigid blew out an exasperated breath. "Please. We hear enough from those who don't eat meat or fowl."

"Really? There are vegetarians here?"

Drawing the hood of her cloak more securely over her head, Brigid responded, "Alastair, my daughter—who has also encouraged the wee lass, Margaret, and Aileen, to name a few."

Gwen laughed. "Then perhaps one of them unlatched the gate."

Brigid's eyes widened. "Don't even make that conclusion in front of the men. My husband found no humor being out in this sodden mess trying to appease an unhappy daughter. She came to him with the information the ducks were missing from their pen.

Nell tends to all the animals."

"It made for great entertainment, though."

Brigid took hold of her arm. Steering her along the pathway through the garden, she added, "I must confess, I watched from another position. If I had been standing where you were, my fits of laughter would have been heard by Duncan, and you don't want to see a Dragon Knight lose his temper."

She nodded thoughtfully. "Are you fearful of the dragon inside of him?"

"Never have I been afraid of the beast which dwells inside my husband."

Halting before the back entrance into the castle, Brigid turned toward her. "I cannot explain why either. In the beginning, the rational, logical side of my mind thought I should flee him. That I should go back to the exact spot I came through time. But I couldn't. My connection with Duncan began long before my journey into the past. From the moment I set eyes on him, our fates were destined. Love has a way of sinking its arrow into our hearts and souls." She sighed heavily. "It's our minds that we battle with the most."

Gwen grasped her hands. "Thank you for sharing your journey. All of you have been so kind. If I wake tomorrow and find I've returned, I will always remember your generosity."

The woman gasped. "Do you believe this will happen? You'll wake to find yourself back in your century?"

Fear seized Gwen. The prospect of a new dawn and being back home frightened her immensely. She released her hold on the woman. "I…don't know."

"What about Patrick? I've seen the looks and

touches that pass between you both. I'm not the only one either."

Gwen's shoulders slumped. She longed to shout her feelings but dreaded the repercussions. Once a truth is spoken out loud, it can never be retracted.

"You love him," declared Brigid, softly.

"Yes." Signed, sealed, and delivered. The truth now set free at her affirmation. "But we are from two different worlds. What can I offer anyone in this century?"

"Besides love?" Smiling broadly, Brigid pushed open the door to the back kitchens. "Let me show you."

Warmth enveloped Gwen as she closed the door behind her and followed the woman.

After picking up a lit candle from a nearby table, Brigid continued onward.

Curiosity hastened Gwen's steps as Brigid led her out of the kitchens, through the long corridor, and down a circular stone pathway. She had never been in this part of the castle. The torches cast an inviting glow the more they traveled along the narrow path.

"There were two of these giant pieces in the chambers which belonged to my husband's mother. We kept one there and made the room a sewing circle, but this one was made for larger work." Lifting the latch on the large door, Brigid pushed it open and stepped inside.

When Gwen entered the interior, she had to adjust to the limited light.

"Hells bells," complained Brigid. "I can never find the other candle holder. I swear each time I enter this chamber, someone else has left another odd piece of furniture or item."

"Is this a storage room?"

The woman snorted. "A place where items require fixing. I need to start a list. Deirdre was the last to be in charge, but after the birth of her son, she fell behind in the record keeping and was thrilled to turn the accounts over to me."

"Her personality is more suited to being outdoors," admitted Gwen, standing on her tiptoes in an attempt to see something in the dim interior.

"Precisely! Along with her combat skills. We were fortunate to have her during a horrific time several years ago. She trained all the women."

Gwen shuddered, recalling the story Patrick had shared with her one evening about the last battle near some standing stones. Her mind reeled at the thought of evil, magic, and dragons actually existing. But an epic battle to save the world? She doubted she could have been as strong as these women.

Returning to Gwen's side, Brigid shoved a lit candle into her hand. "Remain here. I don't want you to trip and injure yourself in this maze. I'll lift off a portion of the covering, but I think you'll be surprised. I've been waiting for the right moment to present it to you."

The woman disappeared behind a towering armoire, taking what little light there was with her. Gwen started forward and then recalled Brigid's words of warning. Lifting her candle high, she studied the intricate carvings on the armoire. The head of a dragon began at the top, followed by Celtic knotwork that traveled down the middle to the base of the wardrobe.

"Exquisite craftsmanship," stated Gwen, tracing her fingers over the carved patterns.

"It belongs to Angus," explained Brigid, stepping forth. "He's having Alastair carve Deirdre's name on the front. It's a gift he's presenting to her on her birthday." She pushed her long braid back over her shoulder.

"How did they manage to move the piece into this room?"

"Very carefully. It was stored in another chamber and Angus considered presenting it to his wife, but only after he had her name engraved on the wood. He caught her admiring it one day."

"How special. Isn't he afraid she'll find it in here?"

Brigid laughed. "Nope. After she relinquished the record keeping, she proclaimed she'd never descend into this part of the castle again. It was too confining for her." She gestured Gwen onward. "Now come follow me."

While Gwen started after the woman, she noted light spilling forth from some candles on a side table. Yet, it was the structure set against the far wall that captured her attention. Her mouth dropped open in awe. "A medieval loom. It's been forever since I've woven anything."

"I knew you would be pleased," declared Brigid, but rushed on adding, "But I must tell you that one of the heddles needs repairing, as well as the wooden beam." She placed a gentle hand on her shoulder. "If you decide to stay, the loom is yours."

Gwen brushed her fingers over the majestic loom while an ache to begin any project filled her spirit. The kindness of these women meant the world to her.

Tears blurred her vision, along with other images. Jamie's whispered announcement. The light spreading out across the giant yew tree and the golden thread embedded in the trunk. As her fingers removed the thread, her steps spiraled around the tree. Light splintered in an arc of various colors, and the world she knew drifted away.

"I need to sit down," she uttered in a hoarse voice.

"Here," encouraged Brigid, tucking her arm within her own. "There's a bench by the table."

Gwen's legs almost buckled. She collapsed onto the rough wood and held her candle outward. "Can't hold on."

Brigid quickly took the taper from her fingers and sat down beside her. "I'm sorry. Was it something I said? Are you feeling ill?"

Wiping a shaky hand over her brow, Gwen took in deep breaths. "No," she whispered. "I finally recalled precisely what happened right before I blacked out."

"And?"

"Jamie told me not to remove the thread unless I was prepared for the other path." The blood pounded in her ears, and Gwen shook her head. "How did he know this would happen?"

Brigid placed a comforting hand on Gwen's. "Out of all the Dragon Knights, Jamie MacFhearguis is the strongest. I don't know the extent of his *powers*, but if he shared this knowledge with you, I'm positive it was for a good reason. Regrettably, it's up to you or Patrick to decipher its meaning."

Unwilling to argue with the woman, Gwen chewed on her bottom lip. "A lump of thread will not sort out this puzzle. Where are my old clothes?" She bolted from the bench, only to become dizzy again. Leaning against the table, she lowered her head into her hands.

"This room is too confining. I suggest we move to your chamber. After you arrived, we cleaned everything and placed it all in the trunk by your bed."

"Thank you." Gwen gasped. "What about the loom?"

Brigid blew out all the candles, except one. "I'll have the men bring it up to your chamber. I'm sure you can supervise them on how to repair the damages."

Gwen grasped the woman's hand. "Thank you so much. I can't begin to tell you how much this gesture has meant to me. And if I may make a suggestion, you need to place Meggie's tapestry back in the Great Hall. It's too beautiful to be hidden away."

"You're correct. It's a subject we women have been debating on how to proceed in urging our husbands to reconsider returning the tapestry." Brigid sighed. "No matter what happens, I hope you'll consider staying with us."

Confused and her mind spinning with her new memories, she asked, "Do I have a choice?"

As they walked out of the room, Brigid answered, "The Fae have always given us a choice, even if the situation appears impossible. Remember, magic does exist. If you'd like, I can take you to the Well of the Fae. We go there often to speak with them. Sometimes they answer, and other times they remain silent."

Gwen pondered the woman's words. And in her heart, she already knew the answers to many of the questions that burned foremost within her mind.

Chapter Nineteen

"Steel the heart. Still the mind. Stop the beating heart." ~MacFhearguis Motto

While he straightened his tunic, Patrick kept his sight riveted to the top of the stairs. There was only one person he desired to see descend those steps. A woman whose beauty rivaled the women here and had stolen his heart. Gwen removed the hardened shield guarding his heart—one he had built long ago. If someone had asked when it occurred, he'd be unable to profess the date. Perchance it started in his fevered condition. Or when his lips first brushed against hers. Slowly, over the days and weeks, Patrick thought of nothing else. Even after he bedded the lass, he thought the feeling would vanish. But the emotion remained.

Each time Gwen entered a room, the light shone brighter and the air grew warmer. Her smile and laughter eased the unrest in his soul.

Though Patrick's mind argued over the possibility of a future, he judged it wiser to banish the negative and allow himself to dream of a life with Gwen at his side. Was not this the season of hope and light? Did he dare to take a step forbidden to him?

Again, he straightened his tunic.

"Why are ye fidgeting so?" asked Andrew, coming alongside him.

Patrick chose to overlook the barb.

"He's waiting for a comely lass to step into his view," interrupted Owain and stepped around him.

Patrick clasped his hands behind him, ignoring the pain lancing through his shoulder.

"Can ye not speak?" asked Andrew. "I believe we have offended the man, Owain."

His friends nodded in unison and took up a position on either side of him. "We shall wait with ye."

Giving them both scathing looks, Patrick took a step forward. Any effort to dissuade them would only result in more prodding. "If ye must ken, I shall be escorting Gwen into the hall for the feast."

Andrew coughed into his hand. "Must be a new custom."

"Aye." Owain chuckled softly.

"Do ye not have somewhere else ye can stand?" asked Patrick tersely.

Andrew looked affronted. "Why? Do ye not enjoy *our* company?"

"Let us give the man his time with the lass," suggested Owain, moving away. "Ye can see her at the feasting. If ye ask nicely, I am sure she will dance with ye."

"All her dances have been claimed by me," warned Patrick.

Andrew raised a brow in amusement. "Interesting." Giving him a salute, he added, "See ye inside the hall."

Patrick resumed his position and straightened his tunic, once again.

Within moments, a vision greeted him. She wore a beguiling emerald and gold gown that hugged all her curves. Golden highlights within her hair flickered in the soft glow of candles, and his mouth became dry. Patrick slowly lifted his hand.

Her smile was as intimate as a kiss with each step she took toward him. When her fingers slipped into his outstretched hand, he drew her close to his body. "Ye are beautiful, *leannán—my sweetheart*."

She squeezed his hand. "And you are striking in this attire."

He leaned his forehead against hers. "If I ken your meaning, this is good?"

Gwen laughed softly. "Most assuredly."

Taking her hand, Patrick secured it in the crook of his arm. "Let us welcome the feast of Midwinter this night."

As she strolled along with him, she asked, "Until the morn?"

Desire shot through his veins. Instantly, Patrick steered her toward an alcove. He had no intention of anyone witnessing what he yearned to do to her. When her back hit the wall, he braced one hand above her on the stone. "I have given ye kisses, but I ache to bury myself in ye again."

Her chest rose and fell rapidly with each breath she took. "I have been waiting each night for you to visit my chamber."

Patrick traced a path along her collarbone with his finger, feeling her tremble beneath his touch. "Have ye?"

"Yes."

Even in the darkened alcove, Patrick saw the flame of passion within her jeweled eyes. He bent his head near her ear. The scent of roses filled him. Nipping on the soft skin, he whispered, "And if I enter your chamber, will ye permit me to kiss ye here?" He brushed his hand across her breasts, eliciting a soft moan from her lips.

"Yes."

He splayed his hand over her abdomen. "And here?"

"Uh, huh," she muttered.

When his hand delved lower, she gasped. "Can I taste your sweet nectar here?" he whispered.

Gwen wrapped her hands around his neck. "You may kiss me everywhere."

His kiss was urgent, demanding. Patrick thrust his tongue into her soft heat. Her moan resonated deep within him as he pressed his hardened length against her body. The air swirled in a tempest of passion as the kiss deepened. No longer caring if anyone came upon them, Patrick continued to feast on her mouth.

"How many kissing boughs have our wives placed in this castle?" asked Stephen.

"In every nook, stone, *and* chamber. I would not be surprised to find one in the stables or lists," replied Duncan.

Stephen laughed. "By the hounds, I do love Midwinter."

Gwen stiffened against Patrick. Placing a finger over her mouth, he waited for the conversation to fade before relaxing his stance and stepping back. Glancing over his shoulder, he watched as the men made their way into the feasting hall. Returning his attention to Gwen, he pulled her out of the alcove.

Her cheeks were stained a becoming pink, and full lips begged to be kissed again. Patrick raked a hand through his hair, doing his best to refrain from backing her inside the hidden enclosure again.

She giggled and stole a glance upward within the alcove. "Yes. We can blame it on the kissing boughs."

He laughed nervously. "This is a first."

"Are you confessing you've never kissed another under these boughs?"

Reaching for her hand, he caressed her fingers. "Never. Leòmhann has seen many a Midwinter feast, but no one dared to place these kissing boughs in the castle."

She tilted her head to the side. Her joyful expression faded. "May I ask why?"

Once again, Patrick was reminded of the curse which surrounded his home. He looked down at her tiny hand. What could he offer Gwen? Why did he continue to pursue her without the promise of tomorrow? Should he confess all to her now?

She squeezed his hand. "If it's too painful to talk about, I'll understand. Let us enjoy this evening and not dwell on unhappy thoughts."

Her words brought comfort to Patrick's tortured spirit. Giving her a weak smile, he brought her hand into the crook of his arm. "Ye are correct. Let us welcome the light of Midwinter tonight."

Patrick's steps slowed as he guided them into the Great Hall. The atmosphere was one of gaiety, laughter, and music. Greenery adorned the entire room—from wooden beams to tables. Children scurried past them in glee, and his heart leaped at the sight.

"My goodness. It's beautiful," observed Gwen, leaning against him. "And look, they've brought Meggie's tapestry back inside the hall. The MacKays surely know how to celebrate."

Within that moment, Patrick made a silent vow that one day he would see the same light enter his home. His heart soared at the possibility, and he nodded the affirmation slowly. *With ye by my side, Gwen, I shall give ye this beauty.*

"Why is there no fire in the giant hearth?" asked Gwen.

"'Tis a custom to wait for the procession of the druids to bring forth the Yule log and light the first spark. I pray our ways do not offend ye."

She glanced sideways at him in surprise. "After everything I've been through? This is a glorious time." Waving her hand outward, she continued, "A time to honor the love of family and friends is a treasured moment." Gwen lifted her gaze to meet his. "And I'm honored to be here with you."

Words he longed to profess to Gwen froze on his tongue.

She nudged him forward. "Let's go join the others. I believe Alastair has been waving us over since we entered."

Swallowing, he nodded.

Rising from his chair, Alastair motioned for them to take the two seats across from him and Fiona. "About bloody time. We thought ye were rooted to the floor. Until all are accounted for, Cathal will not make his entrance."

"For the love of the Goddess, leave it be, husband," pleaded Fiona.

"Gwen was admiring the hall," confessed Patrick.

Fiona brushed her hand over her husband's cheek. "See. I told you so."

Alastair grumbled, but took possession of his

wife's hand and kissed her knuckles. "As always, ye are correct."

She giggled and scooted closer to him.

After Patrick and Gwen settled into their respective chairs, he reached for a jug of mead. "How can the druid ken when everyone has entered?"

"Exactly what I was going to ask." Gwen held out her mug to Patrick.

"Never misjudge a druid," remarked Alastair.

Patrick chuckled while he poured mead into both mugs. "True." Setting the jug back on the table, he lifted the mug outward. Acknowledging each of the MacKays with a nod, he said, "May the peace that resides in this home follow ye to the next."

"Aye!" exclaimed Angus, Duncan, Stephen, and Alastair in unison.

Angus stood. "We are happy a MacFhearguis has joined us on this Midwinter night. Ye honor us with your friendship. May our clans continue to grow in strength and numbers."

"Aye," saluted the other MacKays, each raising their own mugs. After they finished their drinks, each went to take their place beside Angus.

A hushed silence descended when Angus gave a curt nod to silence the musicians. The doors to the hall were opened wide. Within moments, the druid, Cathal, entered. His long robe flowed gently with each step. In his right hand he held a gnarled staff, and in his left, the Yule log. Adorned with greenery, the log would be placed on top of all the other wood and lit by the druid.

Cathal's steps stilled before the leader of the Dragon Knights. "I bid ye greetings on this longest night of the year, Eldest Dragon Knight."

Angus dipped his head in greeting. "'Tis an honor to welcome ye into our home *and* at this feast." He paused as he swept his gaze to his brothers and then outward to those gathered at the table and within the hall. "Generations of the MacKays have fought many battles in and around this mighty fortress. Though it grieves us that our time has come to relinquish our home to another, I ken other generations of our clan will fill the future home—Aonach Castle—with abundance."

Angus leveled a hard gaze at Patrick. "When we leave come spring, Urquhart shall be placed in the care of King William. I expect those bordering our lands to assist our king in all matters. I ken some have heard the whispers, but I received a missive this morning from the king. He has accepted my proposal to see Urquhart remain with those loyal to the Scottish crown."

Patrick gripped his mug, stunned with this new declaration. He understood the Dragon Knights needed to retreat, given their magical powers and the spreading of the new religion across the lands, but to have the king nearby would result in Leòmhann becoming a stronghold in defense. *More reason for King John to invade our lands.*

Angus returned his attention to the druid. "I ask for your blessing over us."

Smiling, Cathal stepped around the Dragon Knight and placed the log inside the hearth. He drew forth from the folds of his robe a small piece of wood. He waved it high in the air, and the bit of wood sparked into flames. After tossing the burning piece onto the Yule log, he turned and faced the Dragon Knights.

The children gasped in delight.

Lifting his arms outward, Cathal proclaimed in a loud voice, "As we greet the longest night, let the light from the stars cast their glow down upon us. The land slumbers, and the battle between the Oak King and aging Holly King begins anew. Though the skies are cold and dreary, we rejoice in song and feasting as this night encloses us in her embrace. For we fear nothing, since the moon and stars will light our path. And as a special blessing, may the Gods and Goddesses continue to favor the Clan MacKay and all those under their protection. Guide them safely to their new home and may prosperity reside there for many years. Blessings of Mother Danu to all!"

A resounding cheer echoed throughout the hall with many pounding their fists onto the tables.

Angus proceeded to pour some mead into a mug and handed it to Cathal. "Thank ye, old friend. Come and join us at the feasting."

Taking the offering, Cathal then took a seat beside Patrick. "I sense wariness in ye."

Patrick laughed nervously. "Ye ken I must bring this news back to Alex."

"Will this pose a problem?" asked Angus, placing his forearms on the table.

"With the threat of King John already on our lands, what do ye think?" He placed his mug down.

Cathal stroked his beard as if pondering something useful to say. "There shall always be battles, a division between kings. Understandably, the Dragon Knights must retreat deeper into the Highlands."

"And this will result in the MacFhearguis clan as a stronghold against any enemies." Patrick frowned and looked at Angus. "Could ye have not waited to speak with Alex come the spring about this news?"

"Truth?"

"Aye!"

Angus picked up his mug and surveyed him over the rim. "We did discuss the possibility of King William taking over at Urquhart. Whether the king stays on here is undecided. But Alex understood what his king was asking of him. The knowledge remained with us—two lairds. Not even my brothers knew of the ongoing conversations with King William. At the time we spoke in early summer, I did not have confirmation from the king. Therefore, until this morning, I was not able to speak of this to anyone." He took a sip and continued, "It was fortunate ye are here, so ye can deliver the message to Alex, along with a missive from the king."

"How did a messenger manage the journey here?" demanded Patrick. "The snows have been heavy and travel not possible through this area of the glen."

Angus placed his mug down. "King William had someone from his *elite* guard bring the letter to Urquhart."

Patrick bit out a curse. He was aware of the elite guards who worked for their king. "Ye mean it was a wolf that brought the missive," he uttered in disdain.

"*Wolf?*" echoed Gwen in shock.

"From the Clan Sutherland," corrected Angus.

"But a wolf?" Gwen drained the rest of the mead in her mug.

Heaving a sigh, Patrick muttered, "Powerful men who—"

Gwen held her hand up to halt his words. "You said it was a wolf. Now it's a man?"

Patrick groaned and looked across the table for some help in explaining that the wolves of Clan Sutherland were an elite group of men trained to be mercenaries, spies, thieves—anything that was required for their king. In truth, Patrick judged them all to be barbarians. Norse fighting blood flowed heavily in their veins. And with the ability to take the form of a wolf, the men were known to terrorize any they came into contact with along their path. Though they fought for Scotland, they bent the laws to suit their own needs.

Patrick drummed his fingers on the table, waiting.

The other women around the table started to snort in an effort to hold back their laughter. And the Dragon Knights kept silent and continued to drink heavily.

Gwen's eyes widened as she stared at the women. "Are they like your husbands? You know...with the dragons inside of them?"

Patrick let out a louder groan.

"Good grief! No," remarked Brigid. "Those men are not like *our* men. They're magical, powerful, *and* ancient, yes. But nothing like the Dragon Knights."

Deirdre turned to Angus and placed her hand on his arm. "Can we hold off from discussing any more clan related business until after the feast? We've gone from merriment to frightening our guest, Gwen. She's been through so much, only to now find out about the wolves of Clan Sutherland."

Gwen pointed a finger at her. "Who roam the Highlands as men, too."

This time, everyone at the table burst out in laughter.

Unsettled by the sudden change in the hall, Patrick slid his hand under the table. Finding Gwen's fingers, he gripped them firmly. Deirdre was correct. This was a night of joy, not worries.

Or talk of wolves.

When she lifted her gaze to meet his, the smile she gave him speared straight to his soul and banished all thoughts, save one.

Loving Gwen.

Chapter Twenty

"Do not fear weaving a crooked stitch. This may lead to a new image and path." ~Wisdom of the Elder Weaver

Gwen shoved his hand away. "Please, no more. I can't eat another bite."

"Do ye not find the fish pleasing?" whispered Patrick, his breath hot against her cheek.

She licked her lips, trying not to look at the man. Between feeding her bites of food and his enticing looks, Gwen found herself almost swooning like a young girl. *After this experience, she would never want to use a wooden spoon again.* "Of course. I taste dill, and I love the smoky flavor, but you've been feeding me continually."

He refilled their mugs. "What about the apple and plum tarts?"

Refraining from any more drink, she placed her hands in her lap. "They're delicious, along with the boar and onions, cabbages, leeks, and a variety of mushrooms—which we helped to gather—and the many sweets and breads." She pushed her trencher away, longing to loosen the bindings in the back of her gown.

"Highly pleasing," he remarked, brushing his hand over hers.

"Made more so with you feeding me," she uttered in a soft voice. The scent of him—all male—lingered in her mouth.

"Tell me more," he urged.

Her face heated further at the intimate tone of his voice. Gwen dared not look at him. As his hand slipped between her joined hands, her skin prickled.

"I enjoyed the sticky sweetness," she admitted.

He leaned forward and dipped his finger into a small pot near the tarts. "Tastes better when sucked from someone's finger, aye?"

Images of Patrick doing wicked things to her body with honey had her pulse racing. The man was intoxicating, creating this tempest of pleasure around them. And she was not immune to participating with her own playful seductive ideas.

"Or other places?" she suggested.

He let out a growl, and Gwen fought to keep her gaze steady on the food in front of her, and not on him.

"I have thought of nothing else but tasting your sweet nectar." His hand pressed intimately between the juncture of her thighs. "Clearly, I have even a better idea."

She chuckled low, trying not to move. The ache grew with each motion of his hand. "The honey would be pleasing."

"*Aye*, mixed with your taste," he stated huskily, removing his hand and reaching for his mug.

Gwen's hands shook as she placed them on the table. What she wouldn't give for a cool glass of water. She took a deep breath in and released it slowly.

Doing her best to settle her nerves, she swept her sight around the hall. The others were either dancing or having their own private conversations. Owain and Andrew appeared to be in a deep conversation with the druid, Cathal. Gwen longed to find time later to converse with the elder. He reminded her of the monks at one of the abbeys near her village. Perhaps he could give her advice on her current situation. Something to ponder in the morning.

My old life seems like ages ago.

Inwardly, she burst with all the happiness life had granted her at Urquhart. Friends, family, and children scampered about in glee. This is what a family ought to be. Joyous and loving. Not like she had growing up.

This is what I've always yearned for. Hear my plea, angels and Fae.

"Do ye wish to dance with me, *leannán*?" His question was playful, but the meaning was not. The man desired her as much as she did him.

This night was their own. A Midwinter to always remember.

Gwen met his lustful gaze. Never in her life had she been so brazen with a man. Patrick stripped the barriers she had kept secured around her heart for most of her life. He made her feel beautiful, desirable, cherished. *Loved.* She uttered the word in her mind on a prayer. Did she dare hope for this from a hardened warrior?

She smiled seductively, her heart racing. "One dance."

His charming smile faltered. "Only *one*?"

Gwen leaned forward. Swiping a crumb from his bottom lip, she whispered. "I'd rather dance with you somewhere else. Away from the others."

His eyes sparked with mischief. "One dance and

then ye take your leave. I will follow soon thereafter."

The deep timbre of his voice rippled over her skin in a pleasurable sensation. "Where shall I go?"

He cocked a brow. "Where else? My chamber."

She pouted. "Why not mine?"

Chuckling low, he winked. "My bed is larger."

"Ahh. Good plan."

Standing, Patrick held out his hand. "One dance, *leannán*."

Gwen slipped her hand into his—a feeling of warmth, strength, and being safe overcame her. And as he swept her toward the others dancing, her heart beat rapidly on this night of light and hope.

****

Unwilling to listen to another conversation with one more Dragon Knight, Patrick slipped out of the hall. Ever since Gwen made her escape from the feasting after their one dance, the MacKays made it their duty to either ply him with drink or discussion. The topics ranged from crops, animals, predictions on the weather, or if he kent where Gwen had disappeared to within the castle.

Patrick would not be swayed. After the fourth MacKay approached him—mug in hand—eager to make conversation, he brushed the man aside. The growing list of lies to explain the absence of Gwen left Patrick in a frenzied attempt to keep them all straight.

Exiting the hall, he made hasty steps down the corridor. When he reached the stairs, he took them two at a time. His heart pounded against his chest as he neared his chamber.

He almost ran the rest of the way.

Upon entering his chamber, Patrick froze. The

shutters had been drawn back and moonlight spilled into the room. Yet, the sight that greeted him nearly undid him. Gwen sat huddled in a thin chemise on a cushioned bench near the window. Her curls framed her lovely face, and her body tempted him beyond reason. Moon glow shimmered off his lass making her appear even more beautiful.

Silently, he closed and bolted the door.

Gwen lifted her hand to him. "Come see the full moon. It's glorious."

Crossing the room, Patrick took a seat next to her. He took her soft hand into his. "I thought ye an angel or a Fae," he confessed, pressing a kiss along her knuckles and inhaling the scent of roses. His thumb made lazy circles over the vein along her wrist, and he felt her tremble.

She shook her head. "I'm definitely not an angel. And how would you know? You don't believe in them."

"I ken they are good. Adam spoke of them often."

"Truly?"

Smiling, Patrick gazed upward. Rising majestically from the surrounding trees, the full moon cast its glow over the land. "Aye. He walks the path of the old *and* new beliefs."

Sighing, Gwen rested her head on his arm. "Regardless, they do lead to good."

"'Tis a beauty, the moon, but it cannot compare to the one next to me," he uttered softly.

She turned around. Brushing a lock of hair out of his eyes, Gwen said, "Thank you, especially for unlacing a portion of my gown before I made my exit. I so love that alcove by the entrance." Sighing, she added, "And you are most handsome, my warrior."

Patrick cupped her chin, soft and warm. He swiped the pad of his thumb over her bottom lip. "I am merely a man tonight. But always your warrior to defend ye."

Her lips trembled. She placed her hand over his heart. "Make love to me."

In that moment, Patrick lost himself with her touch, and he let out a low growl. He captured her luscious mouth, feasting on mead and her sweet scent. Giving his hunger free rein, he eased his tongue into the soft heat of her mouth and teased her. Almost instantly, his *leannán* was playing the dance of desire with her tongue, and he groaned. He deepened the kiss, and his hand trailed a path over the top of her breasts. Her skin was smooth to his touch.

With deft skill, he unraveled the laces on her chemise to expose her ivory breasts. She leaned back, giving him a better view. Patrick wasted no time in feasting on her taut nipples and soft flesh. When he nipped the bud with his teeth, she whimpered. He lavished each breast and then drew her close to his body again. Cupping the back of her head, he slanted his mouth to take more of her full lips and kissed her soundly.

Fire burned within his veins. His cock strained against his trews, aching to bury himself fully into her heated body. Taking his hand, he bunched up the material of her chemise to her upper thighs and sought entry between her soft folds. When his finger delved inside, she moaned deep inside him. He leaned away and watched the play of emotions within the depths of those eyes he had come to love.

"More," she pleaded.

Releasing his hold, Patrick dropped to his knees and spread her thighs apart.

"Wh...*what* are you doing?" she demanded, but made no effort to thwart his movement.

"Did I not tell ye I desired to taste your sweet nectar?" He bent and kissed the inside of her thigh.

She gasped. "I've never...oh, Patrick."

Gwen squirmed under his ministrations, but he held her hips firm. "Your skin is so soft," he murmured, trailing kisses near her intimate core.

Her body trembled. "It's too much."

"Do ye wish me to stop?"

"No!"

With a growl, Patrick plundered her sweet center with his mouth. Her intoxicating scent left him spiraling more with need. He nipped, teased, and feasted on her. Soon, her breath came in short gasps, and when her scream of pleasure echoed throughout the chamber, the firestorm of his passion had reached a boiling fever.

He stripped his tunic from his body and tossed it aside. Standing, he quickly rid himself of his trews. While he stood before her, he watched in a haze as she noticed his desire. Words failed him as he reached out his hand toward her.

"You are magnificent." Standing, she slipped totally out of her chemise.

Grasping her around the waist, he covered her mouth hungrily. The contact of her skin against his own had him almost spilling his seed. His need was fierce, and Patrick lifted her into his arms.

Making quick strides to the bed, he gently placed her on the furs. Lowering himself next to her, he caressed his hand over her rounded hips and took possession once again of her lips. He could lavish them all night long, never quenching his need. His hunger for her was constant. A desire to claim not only her body, but her heart and soul.

Nudging her legs apart, he wasted no time and thrust deep inside her heat. Patrick let out a groan and placed a hand under her bottom. He continued to move within her hot body in a steady rhythm. She fisted her hands in his hair, urging him onward. Powerful, hungry, desire spiraled through him, unlike anything he had experienced.

With each thrust, each kiss, each stroke, Patrick was unable to hold back the tide of pleasure. When his release came, he roared, emptying all he had to give to the woman who had broken down his shields. One by one, all the armor plates came crashing down, leaving him weak and frightened.

A lifetime of sealing out anyone.

A lifetime dedicated to never having a woman steal his heart.

A lifetime building defenses.

And in a matter of weeks, one tiny lass swept in with her beauty and beguiling spirit, to steal his heart, completely.

It was some time before either could move or speak. Gently, he rolled over onto his back and brought her against his chest. Troubled and confused, Patrick considered where their paths would now lead. Clearly, she was sent here for a reason. Love could not have been the motive. *Too simple a solution.*

Patrick caressed his fingers down her back. Cool air drifted in from the open window, and Gwen shivered. She huddled closer against him. He pulled the fur covering over her body and kissed the top of her head.

"Sleep," he urged, wrapping his arms around her.

"Can't," she whispered, lifting her head.

Worry infused him. "Did I hurt ye?"

She rested her chin on his chest. "No, not at all. I don't want this night to end."

"Nor do I," he confessed.

Giving him a seductive look, she asked, "So what do you want to do?"

Patrick raised his arms and placed them behind his head. "We could talk about the weather *or* crops."

She rubbed her body over his already swollen cock and partially raised herself. "I predict snow is on the horizon, and the crops will be plentiful."

He hissed at the pleasurable sensation. Tossing aside the fur covering, he fondled her breasts as he admired the view she presented. "Then what do ye wish to discuss?"

In one swift movement, Gwen surprised him by straddling his legs and taking his hard length into her hands. "How you make my body feel so amazing."

His steady look raked over her body. "Take me inside ye now."

Her body imprisoned him in a web of passion as she slowly eased down onto his cock. His hands roamed intimately over her skin as she moved in a rhythm as old as the Fae themselves. Sweat beaded his brow as he held her gaze. Content to let her ride her passion, he tried to hold back the fervor of his release.

She was a Goddess of the moonlight. Gwen brought the moon, sun, and stars back into his life.

When her cry of release filled the chamber, Patrick

followed with his own violent thrust into her. She collapsed into his arms, and he held her quaking body. Despite their differences, he craved Gwen like no other. Not only in his bed, but also by his side—forever.

Nevertheless, come the morning, decisions he had delayed making for too long required his attention.

Chapter Twenty-One

"Forget the losses. Count only the victories."
~MacFhearguis Motto

Stretching lazily, Gwen opened her eyes. Last night's lovemaking had left her body tingling and sore. The man was insatiable—with demanding appetites. He must have kissed every inch of skin on her body. Never had she known such pleasures or the freedom to try something new. She yawned and turned over onto her side, expecting the man she loved to be sleeping.

On the contrary, the space was devoid of him but glorious sunlight streamed inside.

Bolting upright, Gwen gasped. "It's morning and I'm in the wrong chamber."

She tossed aside the fur covering and stepped onto the cold floor. Raking a hand through her curls, she swept her gaze around the room. Her chemise had been neatly folded and placed near her gown on a chair by the blazing hearth. "Bless you, Patrick."

After quickly dressing, Gwen went to the door and steadied her nerves. Without help from another person, she was unable to fully lace her gown. "Please don't let me run into anyone."

Biting her lip, she eased the door open and glanced out into the corridor. Silence greeted her and she blew out a sigh of relief. Making quick strides to her own room, she froze when she heard laughter. The torches cast their warm glow all around her. Not waiting to see who was approaching, Gwen slipped into her chamber.

She closed the door quietly and leaned against the wood. The laughter, along with muted voices from a man floated away along the corridor.

Shivering from the damp coldness in her room, she went to her bed and stripped the gown from her body.

"What I wouldn't give for a long hot bath," she muttered.

Crossing the room to a table by the window, Gwen poured some water from a jug into a bowl and did her best with her mini bath. By the time she had chosen a fresh gown and chemise, her teeth were chattering. She rubbed her hands together and attempted to tame her curls. Anticipation at seeing Patrick again wove a steady thread of emotion around her heart.

Reaching for her soft shoes, she hastily slipped them on and proceeded to leave the chamber.

Butterflies danced within her stomach as she descended the stairs. Usually, the castle was swarming with life—the halls filled with laughter, shouting, and wailing from newborn babes. Yet, when her foot hit the bottom stair, silence greeted her.

She made her way to the hall, finding only a few of the MacKays' men huddled in a far corner.

Indecision plagued her on where to go next. When her stomach protested loudly, Gwen thought it best to go to the kitchens. Food is what she required. Then she'd look for Patrick.

Smells of fresh baked bread drifted down the corridor, and when she entered, Gwen smiled. Some of the MacKay wives were sitting at a long table, eating.

Deirdre waved her on over. The warmth of this place enveloped her in a cocoon.

Blessed heat invaded her skin and Gwen relaxed. "Good morning." She brushed a hand over Cuchulainn's head in passing.

"It seems you've slept in late, too," mentioned Fiona as she adjusted the sleeping baby in her arms.

Heat bloomed within Gwen when she took a seat. "Tired from all the celebrating."

Deirdre nudged her with her arm. "We all are tired. Some of us never slept either."

Brigid snorted, her face turning crimson. "Nope. We didn't either. It definitely was a long night."

"But a glorious one," added Aileen, smiling wistfully.

Fiona giggled. "But all the children slept. What a miracle."

"Here, have something to eat," urged Brigid, shoving a trencher with warm bread, honey, fruit, and cheese in front of her. I hope you don't mind the small fare. Our cook, Delia, and several of the other women are worn out from all the preparations, so we've given her the day to rest."

"Seriously? I'm grateful for this," declared Gwen. She tore off a large piece of bread. After slicing a chunk of cheese, she wedged it inside the warm bread and smeared some honey over everything. Savoring her first bite, Gwen closed her eyes.

"Long night for you, too?" asked Brigid.

Gwen snapped open her eyes, swiping at a drop of honey near the edge of her mouth. Unbidden, images of Patrick doing wicked things to her body came floating to the surface of her mind. The food lodged in her throat, and she started to choke.

Brigid shoved a mug in front of her.

"No me...*mead*," she managed to blurt out.

"Don't worry," reassured Brigid. "It's water. I believe we've all had enough of Alastair's mead."

"If that were only true of our husbands," blurted out Aileen.

Shaking her head, Brigid said, "Nope. Earlier, Duncan took a pitcher of ale into Angus' solar."

Thankful the conversation had taken a turn, Gwen asked, "So are all the men there?"

Brigid smiled. "Just our husbands *and* Patrick. Apparently, he wanted to speak with them first thing this morning. He had something important to discuss."

Wariness squashed her good mood. Not understanding the ways of medieval men, Gwen couldn't fathom what could be so important that Patrick had sought out the MacKays. And why all of them? Perhaps it had to do with the message from King William.

"You should go take some food to Patrick after you're finished," suggested Brigid. "He hasn't eaten."

Gwen nodded slowly. She resumed eating what was left of her food but declined any more when Brigid pushed another loaf of bread her way.

The women continued to chatter about the marvelous evening. Eventually the conversation turned to matters of what was left for meals and tending to the animals.

Rising from her chair, Gwen prepared a trencher with food for Patrick. "The solar is up the main stairs..."

"And first door on the right," confirmed Brigid.

"Thanks." Gwen lifted the trencher and moved out of the kitchens.

When she neared the solar, she could hear arguing, mostly from Patrick. Her steps slowed, and she hesitated upon entering. Indecision battled within her.

Yet, it was Angus' words that froze her completely, and her meal soured in the pit of her stomach.

"Hence what ye are saying is Leòmhann is not suited for Gwen?"

"Aye, *aye*! 'Tis madness to allow her to enter life with me there," replied Patrick, tersely. "There would be nae happiness, only sorrow."

"Are ye certain this is the path ye have chosen? For ye *and* Gwen?"

"I have nae choice. 'Tis not fitting."

Gwen held a fist to her mouth to stifle the cry. The blade of truth struck with ferocity inside her heart. Patrick didn't want her. Didn't want her at Leòmhann. Didn't want her in his life. How could she have been so wrong about the man?

Her heart shattered into a million pieces.

Deep sorrow cloaked her, along with bitterness and anger. She'd spent a lifetime dealing with those who passed her from one family to the next. Years of pent up fury spilled out in a volcanic rush. She was weary of being told where to go and what to do.

"No more," she hissed outside the solar.

Storming inside the room, she dropped the trencher on a table, the contents spilling everywhere.

Startled by her appearance, Patrick went to her side. "*Leannán?*"

Gwen stumbled away from him. "Don't come near

me. And I am *not* your sweetheart!"

Recovering, he said lightly, "What is wrong?"

"She heard our conversation," professed Angus. "I think we should leave ye both to this discussion."

Gwen snapped her attention to the crowd of MacKay men. "Please stay. What I have to say won't take long."

On a groan, Patrick scrubbed a hand over his face. "Ye do not understand, Gwen."

To keep her hands from shaking, she fisted them into the folds of her gown. "I am not some timid mouse to be told what to do, or where to go, Patrick."

"I never stated ye were," he countered tersely. "Ye have yet to comprehend the curse. Anyone who marries a MacFhearguis and enters Leòmhann shall suffer. Even the land surrounding our home suffers."

Gwen shook her head in utter disbelief. "Stop. I don't believe something that happened generations ago can harm us. I told you this."

"And ye are wrong."

"And you have no faith."

He started to object, but Gwen held up her hand to stay his words. "My life was spent being dictated by others. Fear of not being accepted by my family led me down a path of solitude and loneliness." She dared to take a step near him. "Until I met you. Regrettably, we'll never see how the rest plays out, shall we? You're so determined to make decisions for me that you're blinded by the truth. In the end, you let the fear of your curse have its victory."

Without giving him time to object further, Gwen darted around him and bounded out of the solar. His shouts for her to return filled her head and tears stung her eyes, but she refused to let them fall.

Running into the kitchens, Gwen halted before the women. Choking back sobs, she demanded, "I can no longer stay here."

Aileen came to her side. "Sweet Mother Danu! What happened?"

Her mind was in turmoil, and her heart completely shattered. "I was the fool in believing someone loved me."

"Take her to the Well of the Fae," ordered Cathal, striding inside. "She will find the answers she seeks."

Immediately, Deirdre stood. "I'll take her."

Gwen wiped at her face. "Can we leave now?"

The woman placed an arm around her. "I'll go change and prepare the horses." Turning to the others, she said, "Tell Angus where we're going *after* we've departed."

"Would he stop us?" asked Gwen, frightened the Dragon Knight would forbid her from leaving.

"Not likely, since the Well of the Fae is known only to the women of Urquhart. We are under the protection of the Fae. Knowing my husband, he would want to accompany us. I don't think you want a man along, right?"

"Bloody hell no." Gwen rubbed her nose. "Give me ten minutes, and I'll meet you in the stables."

****

Gray light blanketed the landscape, adding more misery to Gwen's disposition. The sting of the brittle air lashed at her, reminding her of everything she had lost. She'd awakened to a joyful morning, only to have it doused by a terse revelation. She wanted to spew curses at the wind. Scream at all the Gods, angels, and anyone who got in her path. Yet, the words remained frozen on her tongue.

Anger had surged forth and forced out the anguish. Even her parting words with the rest of the women had been brief. In truth, she didn't know what to expect by going to this well. Indecision rattled her completely.

Even the clothing she wore seemed inappropriate. Her jeans and jacket were uncomfortable. The small tunic, modern in style, Fiona gave her was the only reminder of a life she no longer wanted.

"A woman conflicted with the past and present," she mumbled into the chilled air.

By the time they reached a cluster of giant oaks, Gwen couldn't bother to summon a question on what she was supposed to do at this Well of the Fae. Could she vent? Throw rocks inside? Make an offering?

Emotions skidded and swirled in tempest in a varying of degrees. Her stomach clenched tightly like a mass of knotted threads as she fought the urge to double over from the pain.

Guiding her horse along a path bordering the trees, she loosened the reins. She rubbed her eyes with the palms of her hands.

"We can go no farther with the horses," Deirdre announced. "You'll have to walk from here."

On a sigh, Gwen dismounted. Giving a gentle pat to her horse, she wandered toward the woman.

Deirdre took her hands. "Whatever happens, remember the friendships you had here at Urquhart."

"Nothing matters anymore. I have no place left to run," whispered Gwen.

Releasing her hold, Deirdre gestured her onward. "Then remain still and listen to your heart."

Giving her friend a hug, Gwen started down the narrow moss-covered path.

The more she wandered, the more her body relaxed. Even the air warmed. Light filtered through the oak branches, and when she pushed aside the heavy limbs, Gwen had to shield her eyes from the intensity of the sunlight. From gray to brilliance and warmth, her breath caught at the sight.

Despite her exhaustion and conflicting emotions, Gwen was held spellbound by the radiant beauty. Surrounded by giant oak trees, the well was set in the middle of a lush field of wildflowers—from bluebells, foxgloves, daisies, primroses, jasmine, and roses. Clearly she'd stepped into another realm. Bright colors of the rainbow greeted her in an arc above the well, and ivy trailed all around the stones, sloping gently onto the ground. Hummingbirds flitted about, and dragonflies danced in the air.

"A *faery* realm," she gasped, clutching her hand to her chest. Her previous tension eased, and she let out a long sigh.

Drawing near the well, she peered inside. Cool, fragrant water filled her senses, and she longed for a sip.

"Are you thirsty for water or answers?" asked someone behind Gwen.

Startled, Gwen twirled around. She gaped in awe at the woman sitting at a spinning wheel. Her silver hair flowed gently behind her as her fingers deftly moved the golden thread on her small loom. Her lavender dress glistened in the sunlight. Never had she seen such beauty in a person.

Gwen's rational side stepped forward. "Who are

you? How did you get here?"

The woman continued to spin her thread. "You ask questions you already know the answers to." Her hands slowed. "What do you seek, Gwen Hywel?"

"Faery or Angel?"

"Is it important?"

"Just curious," responded Gwen softly.

The woman blew out a breath. "Do you see wings on my back? Again, I ask, what do you seek?"

A tear trickled down Gwen's cheek, and she swiftly brushed it away. "Can I return to my own time?"

"Reach into your pocket."

Confused, she tucked her hands into her pockets. Drawing forth the matted golden thread she took from the yew tree, she brought it up to the light. "How can this help me?"

The woman rose from her spinning wheel and glided toward Gwen. "A long time ago, a group of women made a blessing to the Fae by wrapping a golden thread from their looms around a special tree sacred to the Fae. Their words proclaimed that when a weaver wove the true color on a winter full moon night, the land, stone, and their clan would be cleansed." Tapping her finger to the thread Gwen held, she added, "The clan they spoke of was *MacFhearguis*."

Gwen swallowed, fingering the soft thread. "This is their thread?"

"For centuries, we have waited for the truest of believers. The one who could weave a thread of love around a MacFhearguis' heart. You took a chance by freeing the thread from the tree. From there, you wove the true color of love under the Winter Solstice's full moon."

While she lowered her hand, Gwen's heart grew heavy. "Patrick doesn't love me. Faerytales don't happen for me."

"I speak not of human *faerytales*," stated the woman in a harsh tone.

"Then tell me what to do," snapped Gwen. "If he doesn't love me, why am I here?"

The woman's eyes blazed like the stars. "You speak from a heart that is listening to the mind. There was no curse, but the clan made it so over the centuries. Calm the wind, settle the roar of the ocean, and *listen* to what is the truth."

Gwen turned toward the well.

"Do you love him with all your heart and soul, Gwen Hywel?"

She waited several heartbeats. "Yes. But again, what choice do I have? Obviously, I can't stay here."

"There is *always* a choice. To stay or to leave."

Glancing over her shoulder, she whispered, "And if I want to return back to my own time?"

The light around the woman appeared to fade. "If that is where your heart yearns to be, break the thread and toss the pieces into the well. Ye can resume your life in the future.

"What about Leòmhann? Patrick?" Gwen turned and faced the woman, fearing her response.

The air chilled around them.

A sad smile spread across her features. "My loom is about those under my protection. Patrick MacFhearguis is guided by another. *You* were meant for this journey. Regardless, the choice is yours. You never required my assistance, Gwen Hywel. Seek the path you wish to take. And if you decide to stay, look for the first white rose of Leòmhann to bloom."

In a soft shimmer of colors, the woman and her spinning wheel vanished.

Gwen drew the thread taut, her mind spiraling with bewilderment and sorrow. "Did I not seek the right path?"

Chapter Twenty-Two

"The strength of a MacFhearguis can be found within his heart." ~Patrick MacFhearguis

"Where is she?" bellowed Patrick as he continued to search for Gwen throughout the grounds of Urquhart.

From her chamber to the hall, he searched in vain for the woman who held his heart. Even the kitchens were devoid of anyone, and anxiety clawed at him. Why wouldn't she let him explain? He understood her confusion and grief, but he never had a chance to offer his plan.

Raking a hand through his hair, he bounded out of the castle. "Gwen! Gwen, where are ye?"

His steps led him into the vast garden, searching, hoping for some sign of his beloved. Turning in all directions, he sought out anyone to aid in his search. Someone must have seen where she fled. She didn't just vanish. Or did she?

Patrick's heart constricted with fear. "Nae!" He shoved a fist into the air. "Ye cannot take her back, Fae."

Bounding back into the bailey, he ran toward the stables, almost colliding with Cathal. "By the hounds! Did ye use magic to appear?"

The druid eyed him skeptically. "Your words are harsh, even for ye, MacFhearguis. Ye will not find

Gwen with the horses."

"Forgive me. I have nae time to banter words with ye." Looking beyond the druid, he tried to calm his distress.

"Whom do ye seek?"

Glaring at the man, Patrick clenched his fists. "Where is Gwen?"

"Gone from Urquhart."

Pain as sharp as the sword at his side slashed into his heart. He leaned against the stable door for support. Unable to draw in a breath, he bent his head forward. Darkness shrouded him, reminding him why love was forbidden to him. Raw grief replaced the joy he had welcomed into his heart.

"If ye hurry, ye will find her at the Well of the Fae," offered Cathal, quietly.

Hope slammed back into Patrick, and he inhaled sharply. Raising his head, he asked in a hoarse voice, "Where?"

The druid's mouth twitched in mirth. "Angus had two horses prepared. Follow me."

Pushing away from the door, Patrick paused. "Why did ye not say anything earlier?"

Cathal poked him on the chest. "Ye had to feel the pain of loss before ye were ready to find her." He snapped his fingers and both horses trotted forth from the stables.

Patrick looked up at the sky. "What if she's gone, though?"

The druid chose to ignore his question and mounted his horse. "We travel north through the hills. Do not let the words of the past cloud the present." With a snap of his fingers, rider and animal galloped toward the gates.

Uncertainty clouded Patrick. However, one truth remained lodged within him, firm and strong. He loved Gwen—completely. He refused to believe in another possibility—a life without his *leannán*.

He rubbed the heel of his palm over his heart. "Hear my plea, Fae. Do not let Gwen leave. I need her as much as I do the air I draw into my body."

Giving a nudge to his horse, Patrick took off after the druid.

Onward they traveled—past the loch, trees, and sloping hills thick with snow. Twice, his horse faltered in deep slush and Patrick cursed. Tempering his frustration, he allowed the animal to set the pace. He feared injury to his mount or himself. For some reason, the druid was unmindful to the elements, continuing to gallop across the land.

As they approached a cluster of ancient oaks, he noticed the mists thickened around them. Bringing his horse to a light trot, Patrick swallowed the lump of dread invading his body. A flicker of apprehension snaked through him.

Deirdre emerged from behind one of the trees, blocking his movement. "Men are not welcome here."

"Is Gwen within those trees?" His impatience grew with each passing minute. Ignoring her earlier remark, Patrick dismounted.

She placed her hand on the dirk secured at her waist. "Did you not hear me?"

Unwilling to argue, he looked to Cathal for aid. Nevertheless, the druid remained seated atop his horse while stroking his beard.

Calming his growing fury, Patrick attempted

another resolution. "Lady Deirdre—"

She snorted in disgust. "Kind and flowery words will not gain favor with me."

He took a step toward her. "I beg ye. Let me pass."

"Why?" she demanded.

"My reasons are for only one. *Gwen*." He pounded his chest with his fist. "From my heart to hers and nae others. I waste time speaking with ye!"

She slid her gaze to Cathal and then back to him. Lowering her hand from her dirk, she moved to the side. "Tread carefully, Patrick. You walk on sacred ground, not only for women, but the land also belongs to the Fae. You have already broken a heart treasured by all of us."

Irritable and unhappy with himself, he shook his head. The woman's words struck a wound left open by Gwen's departure. He did not need to be reminded.

Storming past her, he ducked under a heavy limb and made his way cautiously through the dense foliage and trees. With each step he took, his heart raced. Making one final silent prayer he'd find Gwen still here, he moved onward.

When the mists parted, glorious sunlight danced along the ground in front of him. Walking slowly, Patrick emerged into a lush landscape. He dared not move or breathe as he scanned the area, searching for only one.

Unexpected warmth surged through Patrick while he stared at his beloved standing next to the well. His breath caught in his lungs. "*Gwen*." He uttered her name on the breeze.

Lifting her head slowly, she turned and gave him a beaming smile. "Patrick." The tenderness in her expression wiped away all his fears.

Wasting no time, he ran toward her and grasped her around the waist. He crushed her against his chest, overcome with emotion. "Gwen, *leannán*. Ye did not go."

"Almost," she uttered softly.

He drew back and cupped her chin. "I am sorry."

Tears streaked her cheeks. "Please explain, since I am confused."

"I am *sorry* for not speaking to ye first. I had planned on asking the MacKays if—" He swallowed, trying to find the right words. "I considered staying on at Urquhart with ye as my wife. Ye did not hear those words I spoke earlier."

She blinked in surprise. "*Wife?*"

He smiled down at her. "Aye. But I was wrong. Urquhart is *not* my home. Nor can it be yours. Ye were correct. I have lived with the curse over my home all my life. I have allowed the words from long ago to decree a future without love and permitted no one to bring me contentment or joy. To become a hardened warrior was far easier."

His voice shook with emotion as he continued, "I love ye, Gwen. With everything I am and all of my heart. I feared saying the words out loud, lest ye trample over them and my heart. In truth, it was easier to find fault with a curse than to love another."

"I *love* you, Patrick. The warrior *and* the man." Tracing a finger over his cheek, she continued, "I don't know when it happened, but when love entered my heart, peace also resided inside my soul." She choked back a sob. "Even though it was possible, I couldn't go back to a time where I ached for something more.

Where I wanted to be with you here, always. You showed me beauty within me and gave me love. My place is beside you."

She drew forth a clump of golden thread from her pocket. "I risked all to remove this thread from the yew tree near Leòmhann. It led me to you. There *never* was a curse. Only a path taken."

"*Leannán*," he whispered the words against her wet cheeks. "Never leave me. I shall cherish ye always."

"Until the end of time, my love."

Patrick's heart soared. Sealing their vows with a kiss, his mouth covered hers hungrily, devouring the soft feel of her lips.

****

Late February 1210

A warm breeze ruffled the curls around his wife's face while she tried in vain to tuck them around her ears. Patrick continued to admire the view of his lovely wife chatting with the MacKay wives. Their tearful farewells and promises to return—mainly from his wife—had him believing they'd never depart for Leòmhann.

Allowing Gwen this special time with these women, Patrick wandered down to the loch. Snatching a stone from the water's edge, he bounced it lightly in his hand. Contentment filled him for the first time in his life. Now he understood what the Dragon Knights and his brother, Adam had found. Peace within themselves and love for another.

Though it almost ripped apart his soul at the thought of Gwen leaving him, Patrick would walk the road all over again.

Wife. He loved the sound of the word, whispering it

to his beloved many times on their wedding night. His one regret was Alex was not in attendance. They planned on rectifying the failing with another wedding when they returned home.

Kissing the stone, he whispered, "For ye, Adam. May ye and Meggie have many years and bairns to fill Leòmhann with laughter and love." Tossing the stone outward, he shielded his eyes and watched the stone skip four times.

Chuckling softly, he went and leaned against a tree. The water glistened in the early morning light. Geese flew across the expanse of the loch while he watched their flight.

"A missive came this morning from your brother, Alex," announced Angus, striding toward him, along with the other Dragon Knights.

Patrick shoved away from the tree. "His news?"

Amusement flicked in Angus' eyes. "He states that though he is overjoyed to hear ye have taken a wife, he reminds ye of the wager ye lost."

Patrick threw back his head and roared with laughter. "Damn! I forgot."

"Can ye share what the wager was?" asked Duncan, folding his arms over his chest.

"Aye." Patrick rubbed a hand over his chin. "If I did not return within seven days, Alex would have the right of first punch in the lists."

Alastair pounded him on the back. "Ye best prepare your wife that your face might not be so handsome after your brother gets done."

Patrick groaned.

Stephen chuckled. "Perchance ye can make another bargain with your brother."

"Ye ken Alex," countered Patrick. He tapped a finger to the side of his head. "Once a deal is made, the man never forgets. He will hound me until I give in to our terms of the bargain."

"Not even for some of my best mead?" argued Alastair.

"The mead was my plan, not his," responded Patrick, dryly.

"What I would not give to be a witness in the lists at Leòmhann," chided Duncan.

Patrick looked affronted and placed a hand on his chest. "Ye have little faith in my agility and fighting skills."

Alastair wrapped an arm around his shoulders. "Nae, not I. I recall several times ye fighting by our sides. Strong arm and deft skill." His gaze swept outward at his brothers. "Aye?"

Smiling, they all nodded.

Patrick beamed at the men gathered. "I shall miss our conversations. But 'tis time to return home."

"Duncan and I shall see ye in a few months when we meet with Alex," acknowledged Angus. "Until then, safe journey."

Sighing heavily, he extended his arm. "Thank ye. For everything."

After the men made their final farewells, Patrick watched them all retreat back to the entrance of Urquhart.

Yet, his smile broadened further as Gwen hastily made her way to him. He opened his arms wide. "Ready to depart?"

Slipping into his embrace, she hugged him fiercely. "Yes, husband."

Leaning his chin on the top of her head, he glanced at the massive stone fortress of Urquhart Castle, which in a few short months the Dragon Knights would leave.

Their world was changing.

"Thank you," she uttered softly against his chest.

He drew back. "Whatever for, *leannán*?"

"Giving me a little more time with the women who have become cherished friends." Her gentle laughter rippled through the air. "I know you wanted to leave at the first light of dawn. Regardless, you gave me time to tell them what was in my heart. These women showed me that family doesn't necessarily mean blood kin. Their friendship has taught me this—along with a bond I'll treasure forever."

Patrick kissed her tenderly. "I would do anything to keep ye happy, *my love*. Your joy is mine. Ye shall forge new friendships at Leòmhann. With ye by my side, our home will prosper."

Gwen tilted her head to the side and gazed at him. "I love you, my warrior—my *husband*. Let's don't waste another second here. I'm longing to return home. I have a project which requires my immediate attention."

Patrick bent and breathed a kiss along the vein in her neck. "Did I tell ye I have a large bed in my chambers?"

On a moan, she whispered, "Yes, I believe you did mention it—several times."

He nipped the soft spot below her ear. "We have a long journey, especially with the wagon bringing your loom *and* two other companions—Andrew and Owain. Whatever plans ye have can wait until I have had some quiet time with ye in my bed."

She rubbed intimately against him. "Despite your obvious objections, I'm compelled to finish this task as soon as we arrive at Leòmhann."

Patrick groaned and placed his head against her forehead. "Can it not wait?" he pleaded.

Smiling seductively, she played with the laces on his tunic. "I suppose it can, since it will take some time to complete."

"Tell me more after I take ye to my bed and make love to ye."

Standing on tiptoe, she touched her lips to his. "Then what are we waiting for? Take me home."

"Aye," he affirmed, recapturing her lips with a kiss that spoke of more passion to follow, including dreams to fulfill.

Patrick yearned to share many adventures with the woman who had broken down all of his shields. Who banished the darkness with her radiant smile and trusted him to guard her heart.

He tucked her tiny hand in the crook of his arm and steered her toward their horses. "If ye can love Urquhart, wait until ye see the *first* Leòmhann. I challenge ye to tell me where each chamber is located."

"You certainly have my attention. Don't underestimate my prior knowledge of the castle. My memory was faded for a while, but I can now recall everything about the mighty fortress. Even the surrounding area. I was given a special tour."

"Ye have yet to hear my terms, if I win. Furthermore, ye do not ken where my chambers are located within the castle. Your *first* challenge, wife."

Her mouth twitched in humor. "Never underestimate your opponent."

"Then I shall strive to keep ye close."

"How I do love you, husband." Joy bubbled in her laughter and shone in her eyes.

And Patrick's heart tumbled more in love with the beauty at his side.

Epilogue

Leòmhann Castle, Present Day. Midwinter Solstice

Adam observed his wife with growing curiosity as he stood near the entrance of the Great Hall. The woman was fixated on covering every inch of their castle with kissing boughs, evergreen wreaths, and all kinds of ribbon imaginable. Never had he witnessed his home adorned with such finery. Fresh candles found their place in all the holders, and wood was piled high within the hearth, awaiting the lighting of the Yule log.

Inhaling the fresh scent of pine, he strolled inside. "Have ye left any room for the food on the tables?" he teased.

She cast him a stern warning. "Ye mind your tongue, Adam MacFhearguis, or ye shall not be eating the stuffed pork and sausages, or any of the other tempting fare."

"Ye would not dare?" He went to reach for her, but Meggie batted away his hand.

"Can ye not see I'm having trouble tying this bow around the greenery? And aye, I would be so bold as to keep ye from the feasting," she rebuffed, though a smile curved the edges of her mouth.

Standing back, Adam folded his arms over his chest, admiring the view of his beloved and the hall. "Ye have outdone yourself. 'Tis magnificent."

Meggie finished her task and turned toward him. "I do realize there is much in here, but I wanted our first Midwinter feast at Leòmhann to be dazzling."

He grasped her around the waist with one hand and drew her against his body. "How many are we expecting?"

Wrapping her arms around his neck, she remarked, "At last count, thirty-six."

Adam bent to place a kiss on her lovely lips, when her words made him pause. "We went from fifteen to thirty-six people in two days?"

She kissed his chin. "Aye. Surely not a problem. We have plenty of room."

"Who else is coming?"

"Besides all the MacKay cousins—"

Adam let out a groan.

"Stop," she scolded. "Ye ken how much I love them. And ye like them, too. I extended the invitation to more MacKays living nearby, along with some from the ancient MacFhearguis clan."

Adam narrowed his eyes in thought. "Strange, we only recently found out they were living in the area."

Meggie twined her fingers in his hair. "If ye recall, our home was in ruins, and ye have only been living in this century for a few years. I am eager to meet them."

"As am I," he confessed.

"Good," she murmured while leaning her head against his chest.

He glanced around the hall. "Home."

"Can ye sense them?" she asked softly.

Adam understood what she meant, and a shudder of sadness went through him. "Even now, the ghosts of my brothers wander the halls and corridors. They speak to me daily and I to them."

Lifting her head, Meggie touched his cheek. "I love ye."

Closing the door on the past, Adam gazed down at his beloved. "And I love ye. too."

"Sorry, but I'm looking for Mr. and Mrs. Adam MacFhearguis," stated a soft female voice behind them.

Releasing his hold from his wife, Adam turned toward the lass. "Ye have found us."

Smiling, she walked forward. "'Tis lovely to finally make the journey to meet ye both."

A flare of recognition flitted through Adam's memory. "Are ye kin come for the Midwinter feast?"

"Yes. My family didn't know we had any living relatives here. We thought Leòmhann was in ruins. Until we heard from a distant cousin that the castle had been restored."

Meggie stepped closer, a frown marring her features. "Have we met?"

"No. I live in a small village in Glasgow. My name is Gwendolyn MacFhearguis."

Adam's smile faltered, and he glanced sideways at his wife.

Reaching for his hand, Meggie spoke, "Then ye are most welcome. Are ye staying nearby?"

"Truthfully, I have other plans for the solstice. There are ancient standing stones nearby, and I'll be celebrating with other women at the site. My reason for being here is personal. I have something for you both." She clasped her hands together in excitement. "I can't begin to tell you how long our family has waited to present this gift to you."

Without giving Adam or Meggie a chance to speak,

she darted out of the hall.

Neither had to wait long. Gwendolyn returned, along with Jamie. Their son was assisting her with a large rolled package.

"May we place it on one of the tables?" asked Gwendolyn. "It's old and should be handled carefully."

"Of course." Meggie gestured her forward to one of the larger tables and proceeded to remove all the decorations and greenery.

They watched as Jamie and Gwendolyn placed the item onto the table.

Her fingers deftly removed the strings around the material of the long package. "I had assistance from several of the other women this morning." The lass's movements were giddy and animated. "This has been sealed in a box for centuries. We only remove it once a year to inspect for any damage. I must confess, it's in excellent condition for its age."

Meggie placed a hand over her mouth while the woman slowly undid the tapestry.

Adam's jaw went slack. There in vivid detail was his entire family. His sons, himself, and Meggie. All of them resting against the Yew tree of Leòmhann.

"Sweet Mother Mary," he gasped, wrapping an arm around his wife's shoulders.

"Where is Gwen?" asked Meggie on a choked sob.

The lass removed her satchel and withdrew a sealed parchment. "This will explain everything. As for my *ancestor*, Gwen Hywel MacFhearguis, she is long dead. Yet, her vision and gift on the loom, lives on within me. In each generation, a weaver carried on the tradition she started so long ago." She looked down at the tapestry. "Our instructions were to deliver this to you on the Midwinter Solstice of this year."

Tears fell down Meggie's cheeks as she looked to Adam. "She did go *back* in time."

"Yes," confirmed Gwendolyn.

Adam raked a hand through his hair. "Which brother did she marry?"

Smiling, Gwendolyn handed the parchment to him. "I must be leaving. I have a lot to prepare for. This night is one of hope *and* light. I pray I have brought the light to you with this news."

Meggie went and embraced her. "Ye have. Please do return to us."

She laughed softly, placing a kiss on Meggie's cheek. "Most definitely. The group I'm with belongs to an ancient order of weavers. We plan on opening up a shop in the nearby village. We want to instruct those on the loom and such. Evidently, there is much we can share with each other, regarding our families. I look forward to returning here. Now I must leave. So little time left of the daylight."

They watched as Gwendolyn departed the hall.

Adam studied the image of his family woven into the fabric. "'Tis a beauty."

Wiping the tears from her face, Meggie nodded and leaned against her husband. "I'm stunned."

"Open the parchment," urged Jamie.

Adam's hands shook as he broke the familiar seal of the Clan MacFhearguis. He handed it to Jamie. "Will ye read the message?"

Smiling, his son took the parchment.

Dearest Adam and Meggie,

My apologies. I somehow took a wrong turn and became lost. As you must now know, circumstances prevented me from reaching out to any of you. I must share that my life has been blessed, and I'm happily married to Patrick MacFhearguis. We were recently gifted with a beautiful daughter, and she has the coloring and temperament of her father.

Meggie, I made you a vow I would weave a family tapestry by Midwinter. This is my final gift to you, Adam, and your sons—Jamie and Alexander. I have woven the golden thread I unraveled from the giant yew tree into the tapestry. I wanted this to represent the ancient weavers, who merely wanted to send out a blessing. There never was a curse.

And Jamie, be assured I chose the right path. Was I prepared? No. But life is an adventure, and not only did I find the man who stole my heart with love, I also found kinship in the other MacKay women. A truly kind and noble family.

Even though we are long since passed, I pray all of your lives are peaceful and abundant.

Time has no boundaries. Love is eternal. Adam, your brothers' blood lives on in their descendants.

Warm regards,
Gwen MacFhearguis.
P.S. Meggie, I know how much you wanted this, so look for the first bloom of a white rose on Midwinter.

Meggie chuckled softly, brushing her hand over the golden threads around the bark of the yew tree. "Her work is exquisite."

Adam swallowed and shook his head in disbelief. "Ye would think I'd be used to Fae magic and traveling through the Veil of Ages—"

"Aye, considering ye did so too, Father," interjected Jamie with a smile. Placing the parchment on the tapestry, he strolled out of the Great Hall.

Cradling his beloved in his arms, Adam bent and placed a feather-like kiss on her lips. "Have I told ye how much I love ye?"

Meggie moaned and leaned against him. "Tell me again, my love."

Instead, Adam recaptured her lips in fiery possession, drinking in the sweetness of a love that brought him boundless joy.

A Note from the Author

What began as a Highland holiday novella morphed into a much broader story—one that connected the past and present-day Clan MacFhearguis. And incorporating the Dragon Knights (Clan MacKay) meant I was in for an even larger scenic tale. If you've read my stories, nothing is straightforward with these two clans. They dominate every scene they enter, each fighting for control. While they started out as bitter enemies, they are now allies and good friends. With this friendship, there also came loss. I realized both clans still mourned the absence of family members.

This story was one of friendships—new and old—trust, and letting go of previous sorrows. I said farewell to the Dragon Knights of Urquhart. Yet I welcomed a new beginning for the MacFhearguis clan of Leòmhann, and the MacKays of Aonach Castle.

I hope you've enjoyed Patrick and Gwen's love story. Two individuals, broken from tragedies within their families, found the strength and courage to embrace what love had to offer.

What's next, you may ask? I've given you a teaser within this story. I'm delighted to announce that in 2020 comes a brand new paranormal historical series set in thirteenth century Scotland and the Orkney Islands. Mercenaries, spies, thieves, rogues, *and* seducers. These men are known as the Wolves of Clan Sutherland—Protector of King William *The Lion* of Scotland.

Until then, may your dreams be filled with Irish charm and Highland mists.

Other books by Mary Morgan

Order of the Dragon Knights ~
Dragon Knight's Sword, Book 1
Dragon Knight's Medallion, Book 2
Dragon Knight's Axe, Book 3
Dragon Knight's Shield, Book 4
Dragon Knight's Ring, Book 5
~*~
Legends of the Fenian Warriors ~
Quest of a Warrior, Book 1
Oath of a Warrior, Book 2
Trial of a Warrior, Book 3
Destiny of a Warrior, Book 4
~*~
Holiday Romances ~
A Magical Highland Solstice
A Highland Moon Enchantment

A word about the author...

Award-winning Celtic paranormal and fantasy romance author Mary Morgan resides in Northern California with her own knight in shining armor. However, during her travels to Scotland, England, and Ireland, she left a part of her soul in one of these countries and vows to return.

Mary's passion for books started at an early age along with an overactive imagination. Inspired by her love for history and ancient Celtic mythology, her tales are filled with powerful warriors, brave women, magic, and romance. It wasn't until the closure of Borders Books where Mary worked that she found her true calling by writing romance. Now, the worlds she created in her mind are coming to life within her stories.

If you enjoy history, tortured heroes, and a wee bit of magic, then time-travel within the pages of her books.

Visit Mary's website, where you'll find links to all of her books, blog, and pictures of her travels:

http://www.marymorganauthor.com

Thank you for purchasing
this publication of The Wild Rose Press, Inc.

For questions or more information
contact us at
info@thewildrosepress.com.

The Wild Rose Press, Inc.
www.thewildrosepress.com

To visit with authors of
The Wild Rose Press, Inc.
join our yahoo loop at
http://groups.yahoo.com/group/thewildrosepress/

CPSIA information can be obtained
at www.ICGtesting.com
Printed in the USA
FSHW020604271219
65509FS